## "Impressive."

Startled, Mist turned, ready to strike.

Valdyr stood unmoved, the blade mere inches from his chest.

Only years of training had kept her from piercing the blade through Valdyr's body. She went cold at the image of him impaled and bloody. "I could have slain you!" she gritted between clenched teeth.

The small smile he gave her spoke clearly of his doubt, which only increased her ire and the longing to prove him wrong. It was so often a struggle to remember that she was now a child of Christ. Taking a deep breath, she lowered the sword.

"What are you doing here?"

Valdyr lifted one eyebrow at her surly tone. "I tracked the white bear this way." He allowed his gaze to slide over her before fixing once again on her eyes. "You should not be out here alone."

How was it that a man of his size and stature could move with such stealth? Surely his name fit him well, for he was as silent as a wolf and, she was very much afraid, just as dangerous.

**Darlene Mindrup** lives in Arizona with her husband of thirty-six years. She loves studying history, reading and crafting. She and her husband are involved with the Linus Project and spend many hours making blankets for children in trauma situations. Darlene is content to be internet illiterate, although she can be reached through her Facebook fan page, which is maintained by her daughter (who is not internet illiterate).

### Books by Darlene Mindrup

#### Love Inspired Heartsong Presents

# DARLENE MINDRUP

# The Viking's Bride

HEARTSONG
PRESENTS

Recycling programs
for this product may
not exist in your area.

LOVE INSPIRED BOOKS

ISBN-13: 978-0-373-48767-7

The Viking's Bride

www.Harlequin.com

Printed in U.S.A.

Consider it pure joy, my brothers and sisters, whenever you face trials of many kinds, because you know that the testing of your faith produces perseverance.

—*James* 1:2–3

To my Nordic ancestors who passed down
their strength and courage to me. And to my
great-grandfather, Hockenhull Macpherson Gober, and
my grandfather Oscar Cyrus Gober, who passed down
their love of the Lord. I will be eternally grateful.

# Chapter 1

*Iceland, AD 982*

Mist Egilsdottir stood on the crest of a craggy hill warily watching the busy scene below. Her long red hair blew about her from the fierce autumn wind, a precursor to a brewing storm that, from the look of the dark clouds in the distance, was still a few hours away. She slowly took in a deep breath of the ocean air and tried to still her trembling limbs.

The horn warning of an approaching ship had sent them all hastening to the inlet that acted as a harbor for their family farm. For unknown years, glaciers had etched away the land below the water of this fjord, making it perfect for incoming ships. Unlike the waters around her old home in Norway, these waters stayed free of ice year-round because of the strange warm current that surrounded most of the southern and western side of Iceland.

On the banks of the fjord below, her father anxiously awaited the incoming longship coming from Norway. He was still a fine figure of a man, his snugly fitted tunic showing that he was still powerfully built; though his advanced years were beginning to tell on him. His beard had long since gone gray, his eyes slowly dimming. But she loved him, as did her sister, Astrid, who was standing close beside him.

It was because of that love that that ship was now sailing into their safe harbor. On board was the man destined to be her husband. Her heart began to pound with dread, her lungs growing tighter as anxiety shortened her breath. For a woman who had faced death many times without a twinge, it was odd that the coming confrontation had turned her insides into a quivering mass of jelled curd.

The ship itself was impressive, its dragon head lifted high above the water, its planking painted in bold colors that stood out against the darkening sky. More impressive was the man standing at the prow who caught her attention. He exuded power and confidence, things she was decidedly lacking in these days.

Even from this distance she could see the width of his broad shoulders, his stature above most of her kinsmen, though they were no small lot. Also, unlike her kinsmen who took pride in their long beards, this man's blond beard was short and neatly clipped, his honey-colored hair barely touching his shoulders. As he folded his arms, the girth of his muscles was evident in the tightening of his leather vest across his chest. He was an imposing figure of a man. She swallowed hard, wondering if perhaps he was her intended. The thought caused her hands to curl into fists at her sides.

As the ship moved into the channel, he glanced up and his gaze landed on her. For a moment, it was as though they were totally alone in the world, like Ask and Embla, the first two people created by the gods. How long they stared at each other, she was uncertain, but she lifted her chin and straightened her shoulders. She could see the light of challenge enter eyes so vividly blue they were visible even from a distance. Without conscious thought, she found herself massaging her left arm, a habit she had developed since it had been injured last year. If the frown on his face was any indication, he was less impressed with her than she was with him.

When his attention was taken by the young man at his side, she turned away from his disturbing regard and made her way down the hill, away from the harbor. Let her father greet their guest. As for her, she needed a few moments alone to gather her wits after having them scattered to the four winds. Something about the man had filled her with a foreboding and at the same time an unfamiliar feeling that left her unsettled, her heart thumping madly like a war drum. She needed to get away so she could think clearly.

Valdyr Svensson, tired after the long voyage from Norway, was pleased to see the small harbor that meant the end of his journey. He stood in the prow of the ship and allowed the wind to dry the perspiration that was a result of temperatures much warmer than what he was used to at this time of year.

He took stock of the land that would be his home for the next year. The area around the harbor was promising; farther away though, volcanic mountains rose majestically in the center of the island. He had heard many strange tales of this land that others called *fire and ice*, and he was anxious to explore it.

A figure standing on a hillside not far from the harbor caught his attention and he straightened, his eyes narrowing to get a better view. A woman with flowing red hair, her kirtle molded to her tall, thin frame by the wind, appraised him with unflattering regard. As they drew closer, he could see defiance in her stance that, despite himself, his whole being responded to. The blood warmed in his veins, his gaze reciprocating her challenge as he wondered just who the woman could be.

"Ho, brother," Bjorn said, his voice a near whisper at his side. "If you choose to forego this marriage, I will gladly take your place."

Valdyr followed his brother's intense stare and found the reason for his interest. A woman was standing on the shore next to an elderly man that Valdyr recognized as his host and he, like Bjorn, assumed the woman was his betrothed.

The woman was one of the most beautiful he had ever seen, surely an incarnation of Freya, the most beautiful of goddesses. Her flaxen hair hung to her waist, her eyes modestly lowered. She seemed much younger than he had been told, and his father's description of "acceptable" where her appearance was concerned was, indeed, a great understatement. Despite that, his appraisal was only momentary before he returned his gaze once more to the hill.

The intriguing woman was gone. The sense of deprivation he felt brought a frown to his face. Although she no longer stood on the hill, her image was indelibly imprinted in his mind. It had been a long time since a woman had caught his attention and he determined to find out who she might be.

The ship drew to shore and the crew hurried to pull the sail and make it fast while Valdyr and Bjorn swung themselves over the side and waded through water up to their knees to reach the old man and his daughter.

The old man's bearded face creased into a smile. "Welcome, Valdyr. It is good to see you again." He turned to Bjorn, who was studying the presumed daughter rather intensely. Valdyr saw the older man tense, the smile quickly fading. "And you, Bjorn."

Bjorn had to drag his gaze from the woman to greet his host. "Lord Egil. It is good to see you again, as well." His attention quickly returned to the beauty at the old man's side. "And this must be your daughter Mist."

The girl's eyes flew upward, shimmering blue depths steeped with apprehension. Her rose-red lips parted in surprise, and Valdyr frowned, wondering if the girl knew nothing about the planned marriage. Before he could say anything, the old man stepped forward and moved his daughter aside.

"You are mistaken, Bjorn. This is my younger daughter, Astrid." Egil's eyes narrowed at Bjorn's rapt expression, and Valdyr realized that the older man was not happy with Bjorn's interest. Her father turned to the girl and bade her harshly. "Go find your sister and tell her to come immediately."

Hesitating, Astrid eyed Bjorn with equal interest, and Valdyr hid a smile as Egil pushed her with a little more force than necessary. She broke eye contact with Bjorn and hurried off, his brother's longing gaze following her until she was out of sight.

"I am sorry that Mist is not here to meet you," Egil apologized, and Valdyr wondered if Mist might be the woman he had seen on the hill. The thought made his blood warm once again. He was looking forward to meeting this headstrong daughter, who had broken with decorum and refused to meet her future husband.

Valdyr and Bjorn followed Egil as he led the way up to the turf-covered house built into the hill. The front face of the house was made of planking, a rare find here where there were few trees left after they'd been felled to create the farms dotted along the shores.

Valdyr ducked his head to follow his host through the small door and entered a spacious hall. It took a moment for his eyes to adjust to the darkness that was relieved only by the open door, a perpetual fire and a small aperture in the roof for the smoke. The interior of the house was much simpler than his home in Norway, yet the setup was still familiar.

Through the smoke from the fire pit, he could see, lining one side of the house, rows of tightly packed dirt-covered in animal pelts that were used for sleeping. On the other side of the house, there were designated areas for storing weapons and tools, a loom, where a woman was steadily working, and a large wood-framed bed that he assumed belonged to his host.

A long table ran from one side of the house to the other, separating the front of the building from a smaller area in the back that Valdyr presumed was used to house some of the animals in the winter, but was filled now with storage goods.

Several people he assumed to be thralls were scurrying about the hall attending to various duties. The smell of a lamb roasting over the fire made his mouth water.

Turning the roasting spit was a woman who looked like the one who had met them at the harbor. She smiled at them as they passed, and Valdyr wondered if this, then, was his intended. If so, his father's description of her looks as being acceptable was again sadly lacking. Although older than Astrid, she was equally as beautiful.

"This is my daughter Brita," Egil informed them, and Valdyr realized that she was not his intended. Valdyr nodded in confirmation of the introduction, feeling uncomfortable under the woman's steady blue-eyed appraisal.

Egil motioned for them to have a seat at the table, and a young man brought them each a horn of imported mead. Egil stood and lifted his high in the air. "To Odin, for your safe journey."

Valdyr and Bjorn stood and joined him in lifting their drinks.

Taking a long, slow draught, Egil wiped the back of his hand over his bearded mouth and added, "And to the joining of our families."

Since Valdyr had yet to be introduced to his betrothed, he assumed she wasn't present. Frowning, he glanced around at the females but decided that, although some of them were rather becoming, not one caught his attention. Unlike the flame-haired siren he had seen standing on the hill who had set his pulse to hammering.

If she was his recalcitrant bride, Valdyr suddenly decided that the trip might have been worth it after all.

Mist huffed along the narrow pathway through the rocks that had resulted from her constant treks inland. Her father would be upset that she hadn't come to the harbor as he commanded, but this marriage was all his doing anyway. Since she had no say in it, she saw no reason to be involved with the covenant they would be arranging.

If not for her injury a year ago, there would have been no necessity for this marriage. Even now she had tried to persuade her father that it wasn't necessary. Land was becoming scarcer in Iceland as more people migrated from other countries where farmable land was already taken. There was only so much farmable land available here, as well. As a result, raiding had increased, as had land feuds. The peace of the island was steadily being chipped away by the greed that seemed to live everywhere.

Before, her father would have trusted her to take care of the matter, but since being injured in her last battle in Norway and then having accepted Christianity, he no longer had confidence in her ability to do so. Thus the reason for this rather hasty marriage.

The wind caused her woolen kirtle to twist around her legs. That, along with the threat of tears from frustration and self-pity, made her stumble over the rocky ground. Despite the fact that the land close to the fjord was less treacherous, she headed inland toward her favorite place within the realms of the great ice sheets.

She skirted one of the small lakes that dotted the island and reached the small ruins of what had at one time been the home of Christian priests who had lived here in times past.

She had stumbled upon the spot one day when she had been out exploring. The area was a perfect sanctuary, a small green oasis within the rocky terrain caused by a bubbling hot spring that warmed the ground. A slight overhang in the side of a rocky hill created a little cave that hid her most treasured possession. She ducked beneath the small opening and reached to find the cross that had been carved into the wall.

Placing her trembling hand on the carving, she bowed her head and allowed all the feelings that she had been holding in check to come forth. She tried to bring forth the image of a man hanging on a cruel Roman cross but, instead, a vivid image of the man in the boat forced its way into her mind.

*Help me, Lord Jesus. I want to be an obedient daughter, but I am afraid. If the man I saw today is the one my father has chosen for my husband, he is a man who will appeal to that part of me that I yielded when I became a child of Yours and gave up my sword.*

She groaned in frustration, seeing once again that bold challenge in the man's ice-blue eyes, a challenge that she very much wanted to respond to.

*Help me to fight against those feelings that are constantly at war within me. There is no one here to teach me more of Your ways, so I do not know if I am following Your will in this matter or not.*

"What do I do? How can I know?" she whispered.

She allowed her fingers to glide over the Celtic runes that had been carved into the wall next to the cross, and felt once again the awe those words inspired. For years she had not known what they said. It was only when she had brought one of her father's thralls from Eire here that she had found out what was written. In the Celtic language it read, "For God so loved the world, that He gave His only begotten Son, that whosoever believeth in Him should not perish, but have everlasting life."

When the thrall had translated the words for her, she

had felt a place deep inside her open and something had flown forth like an eagle released from bondage.

She had heard those words only once before, in Norway when she was being healed by a monk who had found her dying on a battlefield. To have found them in this small cave had given her comfort that she hadn't felt since she had returned home. Those words connected her to that monk who had not only saved her life, but her soul, as well. To think that men of God had been to this island long before her people gave her a feeling of destiny, a destiny that had yet to be fulfilled.

How long she sat with head bowed in prayer searching for a peace that had eluded her since learning of her father's arranged marriage, she had no idea. It was her sister calling her name that brought her out of the deep meditation.

"Here," she answered, scrambling from the hiding place she did not wish to share with her sister.

Astrid found her sitting on a large rock, chewing on a piece of wild grass, apparently doing nothing more than enjoying the view. Mist lifted one brow in inquiry, noting the ire twisting her sister's face as she placed her hands on her hips.

Mist sighed with no small amount of envy. No matter what mood her sister was in, nothing could thwart her beauty. Astrid's hair was the color of the moon on a cold winter's night, while Mist's resembled an iron sword after it had long been in the elements. Astrid's features were perfect, her complexion without flaw, her eyes the color of the icy-blue fjord, while Mist's mouth was far too wide and her eyes the green color of the lichen that covered much of the hillsides.

Mist stifled another envious sigh. "You wanted me?"

Astrid's vivid blue eyes narrowed. "What are you doing out here? *Far* is furious."

Mist slowly took a deep breath and just as slowly released it as she climbed reluctantly to her feet. She took the extra time to brush the clinging dust from her dress and straighten the brooches at her shoulder. She might as well go back and face the inevitable. It was not like her to be a coward, and regardless of her feelings on the matter, her groom would still be waiting no matter how long she procrastinated.

A thought occurred to her and she eyed her sister with resentful unease. "How did you know where to find me?"

Her sister turned away from her searching look, guilty color stealing into her cheeks. "I followed you one day."

Myriad feelings froze Mist to the spot, not the least of which was the thought that her sister could have been injured. Astrid had found her secret place, but what bothered her most of all was that her sister had tracked her without Mist having any idea she was doing so.

"Why did you follow me?" she asked angrily.

Astrid glanced at her and then away. She shrugged her shoulders, but Mist wasn't fooled.

"I wondered where you disappeared to all the time," she answered after some hesitation.

Mist felt the stirrings of suspicion. It was unlike Astrid to be so inscrutable. She thought about questioning her sister further, but the thought that their father was waiting stopped her. It wouldn't do to make him any angrier than he already was.

She was not nearly as anxious to meet the man who now controlled her future.

* * *

Bjorn was explaining to Egil about the intricately carved knife he was giving to the older man as a gift, when Valdyr saw Egil's daughter returning to the farm with the woman he had seen on the hill.

So he'd been right. She was the enigmatic Mist.

What was it about her that so captivated him? Striding along at her sister's side, she was like a brown sparrow compared to an exotic peacock. Yet she drew his attention without effort.

Egil noticed their return and hollered for the girls to join him. Astrid changed directions with alacrity, while Mist walked as though her feet were weighted by whales. Valdyr hid a grin at her unenthusiastic response, though it piqued his pride no little bit.

"My daughter, Mist," Egil introduced her.

She glanced up at Valdyr, her eyes the greenest he had ever seen.

"My lady," Valdyr acknowledged.

"My lord." The softness of her voice was belied by the hardness glittering back at him from those intriguing eyes.

Egil smiled with satisfaction, glancing from one to the other.

Whatever his host was thinking, Valdyr had the distinct impression that Mist wasn't as grateful as her father for their safe arrival. Her reluctance only piqued his interest further and fueled his desire to see if he could possibly woo her into changing her mind, though why he should want to was beyond his understanding. Perhaps it was the fact that no woman had ever looked at him the way she was doing, as though he were something that had crawled from a bog. Or perhaps it was that, despite her resistance, no woman had stirred his blood as she did in a very long time.

Whatever the reason, her eyes laid down a challenge, and he gladly took it up.

# Chapter 2

The hour was late, the sun finally descending until the light from the open doorway was a mere thread. The smoke from the blazing fire filled the hall until it made the eyes sting and the lungs gasp, yet those in attendance barely noticed.

No matter how hard she tried, Mist couldn't keep her attention from wandering to the hulking Norseman laughing with her father as they sat around the table relating tales of Norway and a freer time before Harald Fairhair had decided to unite the whole country under one king, that king being him.

His eyes crinkled at the corners when he laughed, his amusement making them an even deeper blue. The flickering light from the fire added shadowed planes and angles to his chiseled features. Thor's hammer hung from his neck, the amulet glinting in the reflected firelight. Yes, she could see him choosing the mighty

Thor as his protective god. He had at one time been hers, as well.

When he turned and caught her watching him, heat flooded her face, but she refused to turn away. She straightened her shoulders and stared back. The smile slowly slid from his face, replaced by a look that dared her to…what? She felt the hair on the back of her neck rise in response, her heart rate accelerating until it seemed it would fly from her chest.

Helga, one of their young thralls, brought the mead bag to fill Valdyr's cup once again, and he turned his attention on her, finally releasing Mist from her motionless state. The maid smiled at him, an open invitation that brought a frown to Mist's face. The primitive feeling that surged through her was unfamiliar, and unwelcome. It surprised her that Valdyr turned away from the woman, ignoring her not so subtle offer. Not for the first time today, she wondered just what kind of man he was.

Brita, her older sister, dropped into the seat beside her across the room from the men. She followed Mist's gaze and turned back with a lifted brow.

"Well, well, well."

Catching the meaning behind the words, Mist gave her sister a withering glare, which she promptly ignored.

"He is a fine figure of a man," Brita said as she leaned back against the wall to relax after a hard day. "You've done well for yourself and our family."

Mist sighed heavily. That was the crux of the matter. Were it up to her, and were she not so limited physically, she would have refused the marriage. But things were not as they used to be, and her father was growing older. Brita's husband had been slain last year in the same battle that had injured Mist, leaving their family without any male support except for her uncle and cousins. It was up to Egil's three daughters to provide the family with male protection and male heirs to inherit the land. The thought was like swallowing vinegary wine.

"Why me?" Mist wondered. "Why not you or Astrid?"

Brita's look went to their father, and she smiled fondly. "You know that Astrid is his favorite and that he will not be willing to give her up anytime soon. And as for me," she said, her blue eyes, so like their sister's, darkening with pain, "I am not yet willing to let go of the past."

Instantly contrite, Mist laid a hand on her arm sympathetically. "I beg pardon, Brita. I did not mean to complain."

She smiled sadly in return. "Someday, Mist, I hope to find a man like my Einar and marry again. But not just yet."

Brita's daughter, Erika, came over to them, her six-year-old form barely able to carry the shield she was dragging across the floor. Mist tensed, knowing what was coming.

"*Tante* Mist, tell me about your last battle again," she begged.

Discomfited, Mist's look flew to Valdyr. He glanced from Erika to Mist, one brow winging upward in question.

Brita hurriedly tried to divert her daughter's attention. She pulled the heavy shield from Erika, grinning at her child's relief as she was assuaged of her burden.

"Let us not bother *Tante* Mist tonight, *elskling*."

"But *Mor*," she whined. "I want a story."

"I would like to hear one, as well," Valdyr interjected. His assessing gaze moved from the top of Mist's fiery crown of hair to her dirty bare feet peeking from beneath her kirtle to her eyes, where his regard held steady.

"The shield is yours?"

Mist bristled at the disbelief in his voice. Before she could answer him, her father spoke up.

"Mist is a shield maiden," he informed him, the pride evident in his voice.

Valdyr's shocked expression did nothing toward improving her already deflated ego. How could a man so strong and virile possibly understand her shortcomings? Had he ever been so severely injured that he almost died? She knew little about him, but she sincerely doubted it. He radiated an aura of power that was truly intimidating, and it embarrassed her to seem so lacking in his eyes.

Valdyr watched the color sweep across Mist's face. He couldn't have been more surprised if they had told him that the woman had two heads, although he supposed he shouldn't have been. Hadn't he recognized the hidden fire in her even from a distance? It would take a woman of such passion to be a shield maiden. He had come across few in his time, but they had left an indelible impression on him.

"Not is. Was," Mist corrected her father.

He found it hard to believe that the woman could pick up a heavy sword, much less wield it. Although tall, she was so thin that the bones protruded from her shoulders, her upper torso lacking the muscles he would expect to see in such a one. He had noticed earlier that she favored her left arm and that she was often unconsciously massaging it.

"Was?" he queried, intrigued. Egil had said nothing of this when he had come to make the marriage arrangements.

Egil spoke up in his daughter's place. "Mist fought against Harald at the Battle of Hafrsfjord. She was seriously injured and has yet to recover fully."

He sounded almost apologetic, as though he had tried to pawn off damaged goods. Valdyr glanced sympathetically at Mist's left arm. She lifted her chin defiantly.

"An opponent's ax went through my shield and…and damaged my arm."

Brita snorted derisively. "It did more than just damage her arm. It nearly took her life."

Whatever the others wanted to say, Mist silenced them all with a look. Brita got up to tend to the cooking, and Egil suddenly took an intense interest in sharpening his sword.

Something was being left unspoken. Whatever it was, he would find out in time, before this marriage took place. He gave Mist a look that said as much, and he watched curiously as the little color there drained from her already-pale cheeks.

To relieve the tension, he turned to Erika. "Perhaps you would like to hear a story from my brother instead. He is very good at telling stories."

Bjorn gave him a look that brought forth a chuckle. Valdyr hadn't missed his brother's attempts to woo young Astrid with tales of his own. It amused him that the girl acted so unmoved by him, yet the look in her eyes spoke clearly of her interest. Seeing their youthful inexperience in matters of romance made him feel every one of his nearly thirty years.

Easily diverted, the child crossed the room, and Astrid motioned for her to crawl into her lap. As Bjorn began his tale, Valdyr seated himself next to Mist.

"This is not your shield, then?" he asked, pointing to the one Brita had set aside.

Mist shook her head, her eyes softening as she looked at her niece. "No. It belonged to Erika's father."

"Tell me about him," Valdyr invited, sensing a story.

Her green eyes plumbed the depths of his, as if trying to find the reason behind his interest. Whatever she saw must have reassured her. She drew her legs up under her, settling her chin on her upraised knees.

The flame from the fire reflected in her flowing mane, giving it the illusion of being on fire itself. Valdyr wanted to reach out and touch it, but her next words brought his thoughts to a slamming halt.

"Einar came here with father during the *landnám*. Even as children, he and Brita were inseparable. When they were old enough, father gave his permission for them to marry. It was Einar who taught me to fight."

Those green eyes turned back to him, and he found himself swallowing down unreasonable jealousy. It would have taken hours of training for her to become skilled enough to wield a sword in battle, which meant that she had spent many hours with this Einar.

"Your sister didn't mind that he chose to teach you instead of her?" He would never allow another man to spend so much time with his wife.

She frowned in puzzlement. "Brita had no desire to learn to fight. She was content being a mother."

"And you?" Valdyr asked. "Do you not wish to be a

mother?" His own mother certainly hadn't. He glared at Mist, wondering just what kind of woman he had agreed to marry.

She turned so that he could not see her face. "Father was getting older and he had no sons. Then when Brita had a girl child, as well, I decided that someone needed to be prepared to fight and that motherhood wasn't in the runes for me."

There was a strange tone in her voice that led him to believe she was not as unmoved as she tried to appear. He leaned back against the earthen wall and studied her curiously. "The two are not mutually exclusive."

Her face set grimly. "They are for me. As a mother, my first thought would always be for my children. When in battle, my first thought must be to survive. A warrior cannot have a divided mind."

She turned those fascinating eyes on him once again and the room grew suddenly overwarm.

"I know what it is like to grow up without a mother," she told him.

There was something in her voice that spoke more clearly than words of the pain and regret of her past. He empathized with that pain. If his own mother had been like Brita, or even Mist, how much different would his life have been? His fingers itched to reach out and comfort her with a touch, removing the pain he saw in her eyes. Instead, he curled them into fists to keep from doing any such thing.

Mist winced under his intense scrutiny. She knew what she must look like. She was a pale shadow of the woman she used to be. Being close to death had left a lasting impression on her.

It had taken her months to heal. Every day she had prayed to the goddess Hel to take her to Valhalla, the afterworld of fallen warriors, or to Niflheim, the cold, icy netherworld of all others. She cared not which, as long as it would relieve the mental suffering that was worse than physical pain. To live life as a cripple was unacceptable. Her family did not need a useless person to care for.

Every day the monk Drustan had prayed to his God for her life, and every day she prayed that Hel would overcome his God and show just who was superior. In the end, it was Drustan's God who won out.

Drustan had emigrated from Eire to Norway to, as he said it, preach to the heathen. From all of his accounts, she was one of the chiefest. A soft smile curved her mouth as she remembered their fierce verbal battles between her prayers to Hel and his to his God. He had refused to give up on her.

After a time, her body began to heal and she became intrigued by the Christian God. Drustan taught her about the words that his God had left in writing to show mankind the way to Him. The words from his scrolls embedded themselves in her mind. *For the word of God is living and active and sharper than any two-edged sword.* As a warrior, those words had arrested her attention more than any of the other things he had read. She would give just about anything to be able to read those scriptures for herself.

He also told her about a heaven that was filled with light and goodness, and she began to yearn for such a place. When she had asked why he didn't just let her die and go there, he had told her that no one could go there except through Jesus, the Christ.

After that, she had been baptized and he had continued to teach her until she was well enough to go home to her family. A part of her had resisted the thought of leaving Drustan's safe haven, but her family needed her. With Einar dead, they had no one else to protect them.

She had arrived home more bones than skin after the intense struggle for her life, and she had yet to fully regain her girth. The muscles in her arms that had once been strong and supple had weakened without use.

Now this man sat here in vigorous health with muscles any woman, or man for that matter, would envy, and she felt her inadequacies. The darkness of his skin and the lightness of his hair spoke of much time in the sun. He exuded pure masculine strength. A man like him would have no time for a weak wife.

Her eye caught the glint of the amulet hanging around his neck, and she realized that he would consider her fledgling faith another weakness. Her people had no time for a God who spoke of love and forgiveness, despite the fact that Harald had claimed Christianity for Norway and insisted on the people being baptized.

As Drustan had told her, it was one thing to say you were a Christian, and quite another to actually practice it.

"So, Valdyr," her father called, interrupting her thoughts. "Are we agreed that the marriage will be at the next autumn solstice?"

Mist met Valdyr's eyes, and the fire in his nearly stopped her breathing. A slow smile curled his lip.

"Make the arrangements."

Mist lay next to her sister. All the breathing and snoring going on in the house was louder than the thunder from the storm that had passed through earlier. With the arrival of Valdyr and his men, the house had become decidedly cramped. Bodies were sprawled over just about every inch of the floor, as well as on the packed earthen bedding that ran along the walls.

Restless, she got up and picked her way among the sleeping bodies and, pulling a cloak from the peg by the door, she slipped out into the night.

The long darkness had yet to begin but already the air had taken on a chillier feel. Though it was the middle of the night, the sun hung low on the horizon, giving just enough light to show her the way to her favorite spot overlooking the fjord.

She seated herself on the springy turf regardless of the moisture clinging to the grass and curled her legs under her. She loved to come here when the others were asleep and commune with her Lord, forgetting the past and concentrating on the present and possible future.

Before, that future was keeping her family safe. Now, that would no longer be the case.

What frightened her more than anything was the fact that she didn't know how to be a wife. Her mother had died when she was little and the only example she'd had was Brita, but Brita had been married such a short time before her husband was slain, and Brita had married for love.

A rock tumbling down the hill startled her. She turned, half rising to her feet, when she saw Valdyr's massive form making his way toward her.

He motioned for her to stay seated, and she eased back to her position though she was far from relaxed in his presence. She fixed her gaze on the sun's dim reflection on the fjord's waters. The nearer he drew, the faster her heart beat. She tugged the robe closer about her and willed her breathing to slow.

"Did I waken you?" she asked.

He seated himself beside her and every nerve in her body jumped to life. He bent his knees, resting his muscled forearms on them, and followed the direction of her interest.

"No. I couldn't sleep."

She didn't have the courage to ask what was on his mind. Frankly, she wasn't certain that she wanted to know.

They sat for some time, the silence growing uncomfortably long.

Valdyr finally leaned back on his arms, his leather jerkin tightening across his broad chest, and cocked his head toward her. "Is this marriage agreeable to you?"

What was she supposed to say to that? One part of her admitted to the strange attraction she felt for the man sitting beside her; the other, more sane part knew that their two competing faiths and strong wills were bound to cause conflict.

Her people were a passionate, heathen race, living their lives in a primeval way that had remained unchanged for many, many years. Even she, before she had accepted the Christ, had lived in such a way, her primitive nature reveling in her successes in battle that even now brought a quickening of her blood.

She glanced at him. "Did my father tell you that I am a Christian?"

His eyes narrowed, and he studied her for several seconds. "No, but I do not see that that is a problem. Most people in Norway have been baptized to accept the Christian faith."

That was certainly true enough, even though for the most part it was because Harald demanded it.

"Even you?"

His lips thinned, and he turned back to watching the fjord. "No. I would never accept such a weak god."

So, then, did he see her as weak because she had? She wished that she could talk to Brother Drustan. If only she knew what God's word said, she would better be able to answer all the questions that were plaguing her mind.

She had at one time been known as Mist *in karlsefna*, Mist the he-man, and she had been proud of that title. Now, she was called Mist *in Kristna*, Mist the Christian, and not in a flattering way.

The more she studied the man beside her, the more she realized that she was not the right woman for him. Perhaps the woman she used to be would have gladly fallen into his arms, but she was no longer that woman because of her faith.

She didn't realize that she had spoken her thoughts aloud until he turned to face her, a frown forming a deep V between his brows.

"What are you saying? Do you find something objectionable about me?"

What was she supposed to say to that? That she feared that primeval Viking male in him that appealed to the primitive part of her Viking nature, the part she was daily trying to fight into subjection? She could feel the threads of attraction trying to pull her ever closer to him. It was as though a dark force outside herself was trying to woo her into forgetting the new life she had accepted in Christ. It was not the Viking way to retreat from a dangerous situation, but Mist decided, in this instance, retreat was the better part of valor.

"Perhaps we can discuss this another time. The hour is late and I find that I am tired after all."

Mist started to get to her feet. Reaching out, Valdyr gripped her wrist and held her in place. It dented his pride considerably that after fending off advances from so many women through the years, this woman, who had attracted him from the start, not only didn't give any encouragement, she was actually discouraging him.

She glanced pointedly at his fingers, the warning in her eyes bringing an instant desire to test her. Did she really think that she could best him if he took up her challenge?

At the same time, he sensed a vulnerability about her that was in direct contrast to the strong woman she was trying to portray. Which was the true Mist? If he pushed her now, she might very well retreat into a place he could not access. The one thing he had right now was time. Well and good. He would give her that time.

He released her, and she hastily climbed to her feet, brushing the wet grass from her tunic. She gave him a look fraught with meaning that almost brought him to his feet, but he forced himself to remain still and not take advantage of it. The yearning in her eyes was plain to see and encouraged him to believe that with time and patience he could win her over.

The only problem with that thought was he found he was decidedly limited on patience where she was concerned.

## Chapter 3

Mist awakened to the sound of clanking pottery as Brita prepared the meal to break the fast. Light from the open door spoke of the sun's having already risen high in the sky. She had slept much later than she'd intended, having spent a restless night tossing and turning, her dreams intermittent, all of them about Valdyr.

She sought the place where Valdyr and his men had made their beds but the area was empty and the pallets had already been removed to allow for the daily jobs that needed tending. Most of the thralls who helped with the inside work had always made their bed in the longhouse with everyone else. With the coming of Valdyr and his men, they had been relegated to the smaller longhouse with the field thralls. Valdyr and his men required a lot of room.

She shivered as the early-morning cold blew in the open door. She quickly rose to help her sister with the meal, throwing her apron over her kirtle and pinning it at the shoulders with her favorite brooches.

Her father's thralls were already busy about their chores. Gudrun was deftly spinning the wool that would be used to make new clothing. Standing for hours as the wool was spun by dropping weights from the shoulder was backbreaking work, yet Gudrun seemed to enjoy it. She had told Mist that it allowed her time to think. Mist could only wonder what the woman thought about; she rarely spoke to anyone.

Ari, a young man who had been purchased by her father several years ago, was bringing in wood that had been hauled to the farm from farther inland. He had barely seen fifteen years and, despite the fact that he was a slave, he was a joy to be around. Mist was thankful that his longing for his home in Northumbria dwindled with each passing day, but she couldn't help but sympathize with his situation.

Drustan had told her that slavery was wrong. She could well understand why. God's holy word said that others should be treated as you would wish to be treated yourself. For her part, she would rather be dead than be someone's thrall. She had tried to make her father see that, but it was futile, as were all of her other attempts to teach him about the Christian way. As for herself, she had determined that she would never own a slave.

Which brought her thoughts back around to Valdyr. He would be the head of their house, so she would have to find out how he felt about slavery, because it was an area she refused to compromise on.

She joined Brita at the table where she was cutting slices of cheese and putting them on a wooden platter.

Brita glanced at her. "*God morgen*. Did you sleep well?"

Since Mist didn't want her sister worrying, she told her, "Well enough. What can I do to help?"

"Find Astrid," she responded immediately, exasperation evident in her voice. "She rose early and I haven't seen her since. She is supposed to be carding the wool for Gudrun."

Mist lifted a slice of cheese from the platter, saluted her sister with it and proceeded outside.

She stood waiting for her eyes to adjust to the bright light after the darkness of the house. Already the farm was alive as everyone went about their chores. Several thralls were already preparing the field for a second harvest of barley. With the hours of daylight here so long, they were often able to get up to three harvests a season.

Her aunt was busy in the garden behind the house, tending the vegetables. "Have you seen Astrid?"

She slowly straightened from her cramped position, placing one hand at her lower back. Pushing back the gray hair that had escaped from her braid, she pointed in a direction away from the farm.

"I saw her earlier. She went that way."

Mist grew suddenly uneasy. Why was her sister going inland when she knew there was work to be done?

"Was she alone?" Mist asked.

Her aunt nodded and then turned back to her work. The foolish girl. Anything could happen to her wandering alone out there. An immense white bear had been spotted near the farm and some of the sheep had come up missing, their mangled bodies found farther inland where the bear must have made its home.

"Thank you, *Tante* Adisa," she told the older woman.

She sighed. There was no help for it. She would have to go after her.

She hurried back to the house and went to where they kept their stored weapons. Since she had yet to regain the full strength of her arms, she chose a smaller, light-weight sword and slipped the baldric over her shoulder, settling the end against her waist.

Deciding to add a spear to her arsenal, she again chose one that was lighter in weight than what she would have preferred. It suddenly occurred to her that choosing to give up her sword was not a wise thing to do. There were other creatures besides man that were a threat to her family. She decided then and there that it was time to begin practicing again.

She passed the thralls who were building a rock wall to surround their farm and its outlying fields. They waved and she waved back. Unlike her father, she thought of the thralls as her friends rather than slaves, and they responded to her in kind.

She searched for her father, but he had left earlier to show Valdyr and Bjorn around the farm. Leaving a message for him with one of the thralls that she would return soon, she quickly went in search of her sister. She didn't dare mention Astrid to anyone. Her secre-tive actions lately had caused Mist concern. She should have confronted her sister long ago, but she had been too caught up in feeling sorry for herself.

The rain from the night before had freshened the air, and she took a deep, cleansing breath after hours in the smoke-drenched house. She stretched, easing the kinks out of her body, and a scripture that Drustan had taught her came to her mind. It was from the book of Jeremiah, the prophet, and it said that if one searched for God with all of one's heart, He would be found. A strange sense of contentment stole over her as she traveled farther inland.

It soon became apparent from her tracks that Astrid had gone to Mist's refuge spot again. Mist grew unreasonably irritated. She had jealously guarded the spot from prying eyes, but she couldn't begin to explain why. Perhaps she was afraid that if her father knew about it, he would destroy it. He had not been particularly happy about her conversion to Christianity.

Before Mist reached the rock formation that housed her little sanctum, she could hear voices raised in heated anger. She quickly rounded the bend and stopped in amazement as she found her sister and a young man embroiled in some sort of argument. It took her a moment to sort out the scene, but then she recognized the son of the chief of the farm many miles away. Anger surged through her, her hand tightening on her spear.

"What are you doing here, Balder?"

He lifted his chin, straightening to his full height, which, even for her people, was considerable. His handsome face was marred by the fierce frown he leveled at Mist.

"I am here to see Astrid."

Her sister's guilty look made it clear that this was obviously no chance meeting.

"And why is it necessary that you two meet in secret?" Mist asked. Balder's eyes went from the sword hanging from her shoulder to the spear clenched tightly in her hand.

Astrid spoke. "I was just telling him that I would no longer meet him here."

Balder growled an objection to her words, and Astrid

took a hasty step in retreat. Mist stepped between them, her glaring eyes a direct challenge.

"You have some disagreement with that?"

Again Balder's eyes went to her sword. Mist's reputation as a shield maiden was well-known on the island. The look on Balder's face assured her that he had yet to learn of her weakness. Thankfully, this gave her the advantage. Balder swallowed hard, his face creased with frustration.

Mist turned to her sister, keeping one eye on the angry young man beside her. "Go home. You are needed." As Astrid turned to obey, Mist told her, "We will talk about this later." Her sister's shoulders dipped with remorse, and Mist knew she was already regretting her clandestine affair. More than likely a good part of that had to do with Bjorn.

She turned back to Balder and, despite the fact that she had never really liked the young man, she was grieved that he had to be hurt. "Go home, Balder. If my father sees you near our farm, it will not go well with you."

Before the arrival of the bear, her father's herds had been raided and he had suspected that it was Balder's clan that was doing it. What was her sister thinking meeting him here? And how had she even managed to get to know the boy in the first place?

Nostrils flaring in anger, Balder looked like he was about to object. Mist slightly lifted the spear, her warning evident.

He hesitated, his dark blue eyes glittering with malice. Grabbing the cloak that he had discarded on a rock nearby, he glared hard at Mist. "This is not over yet," he said. He turned on his heel and stormed away.

Mist let out a relieved breath and watched until he was out of sight. She quickly scanned the area around her. It had always given her pleasure to know that she had a spot that was unknown to others, a seemingly pristine sanctuary where she could retreat from the world. Now it seemed to have been desecrated. She didn't think she would ever think of this place the same way again.

Sighing, she followed her sister home, her thoughts in a tangle. Balder somehow made her think of Valdyr, though truth to tell, the two were as different as night and day. Both were strong and determined, but Valdyr seemed the more reasonable of the two. She had noted the same strange possessive look in Valdyr's eyes last night as she had seen in Balder's today, yet she could not imagine Valdyr being as violent. But, then again, not having the same beauty as her sisters, she couldn't imagine that her looks would ever inspire such a great passion in a man, either.

Valdyr looked up from watching the blacksmith forging the iron that Valdyr had brought as a gift to Egil and saw Astrid come storming into the compound. Eyebrows lifted, he glanced at Bjorn, who looked equally surprised. Shrugging, he turned back to the forge. A moment later, Mist followed after her sister, a sword slung in a baldric over her shoulder and a spear in her hand. The look on her face boded ill for the recipient.

Once again his brows lifted in surprise. Egil had told him that since his daughter's return from the battle in Norway, Mist had given up her sword. Seeing her fully armed and in an obviously savage frame of mind, he quickly made his way to her side.

Head bent, she was so focused on her thoughts that she didn't even see him until she rammed into him. He gripped her shoulders to keep her from tumbling to the ground. Palms against his chest, she stared up at him in surprise.

He glanced behind her and then fixed an inquiring gaze on her face. "Is everything well?"

"Everything is well," she told him, trying to push out of his hold.

Strangely reluctant to let her go, he held her more firmly. "Then why the weapons?"

Instead of fighting him, she softened her stance. "Our men spotted a white bear close to the farm. Astrid foolishly went afield without protection."

He studied her face, only half hearing what she said. He could feel the bones protruding from her shoulders, the seeming fragileness of her making him feel suddenly protective. Truth be told, she couldn't be considered a comely woman. In fact, her features were quite unremarkable, especially compared to her sisters. So what was there about her that so intrigued him?

"And what did you intend to do with *those* weapons? Tickle him?"

The sword was child-size, the spear so light it would take a great amount of power to penetrate a rabbit much less the thick skin of a white bear. Surely the woman had been moonstruck if she thought to go up against a bear so ill equipped.

She gave him a look that would have quelled a lesser man. He could see in her eyes that she knew he spoke the truth and it frustrated her. Whatever she had been capable of before, she could no longer match him, or any other man.

Pushing his hands from her shoulders, she glared at him briefly before she started to walk away. He moved into step beside her.

"Just so you know, we intend to go out looking for the bear. It needs to be slain before any more sheep go missing."

She stopped, turning to glance back the way she had come, a frown drawing down her brows. He caught her look of misgiving before she turned and walked on.

What had concerned her? He didn't need to remind her that even though her father was one of the wealthiest men on the island, his wealth was bound up mostly in his livestock. It didn't take much to see that with all the profitable land being taken, the only way for their wealth to grow would be from outside sources.

It was the reason for this marriage agreement. His family would benefit from the land here in Iceland, and her family would benefit from his father's resources. Their fathers had been friends for years, fighting and raiding together. It had been their greatest wish to join their families someday. Egil had yet to produce a male heir, and it was doubtful that he would this late in his life. He was afraid that his brother would by default become *godar* in his stead, taking Egil's daughters' inheritance. By marriage, Valdyr would take his place as chieftain when the time came and prevent that from happening.

At first, Valdyr had balked at the idea of an arranged marriage, but his dissatisfaction was fast receding.

Iceland would be a good place to raise a family, where the people were free to live their lives away from kingly rule. It had been one of the things that had drawn him here, a willing participant in an unwilling alliance. Un-

willing at least as far as Mist was concerned. He brushed
that thought aside. Winning her over would be a challenge, and he was definitely up for a challenge.

"When will you leave?" she asked him, turning his
thoughts back to the moment at hand.

"Soon."

She turned to face him before entering the house, and
folded her arms while blocking his path. "Then, pray,
do not let me keep you."

He grinned. Reaching past her, he pushed the door
wider to allow them both entrance. "I would not think of
it. *After* I break the fast," he told her, and with his body
nudged her slight frame to the side, leaving her on the
threshold. He could almost feel her fuming look pierce
his back as she followed him in.

They both paused inside the doorway until their eyes
adjusted to the darkness before heading in opposite directions.

Valdyr watched her cross to the fire, a slight smile
curling his lips. He wondered, not for the first time, just
what Mist would have been like in full, robust health. If
the heat in her gaze at times was anything to go by, she
must have been a force to be reckoned with.

Mist joined her sisters at the fire. Brita smiled at her,
but Astrid turned away and hurried across the room to
help Gudrun. She could run, and she could hide, but they
*would* have a talk before this day was through.

Brita lifted a brow in question.

"I will explain later," Mist told her.

Nodding, Brita placed the food out and called to the
men. They quickly made their way to the table, hungry
from the long night's fast. Mist smiled as they fell upon

the food with ravenous appetites. Her sister had done herself proud for their visitors.

When everyone's attention was fixed elsewhere, Mist made her way to Astrid's side.

"I need to speak with you outside."

Seeing the objection on her sister's face, Mist lowered her voice even further. "Now."

Astrid reluctantly rose. Gudrun glanced at them curiously but remained silent, continuing on with her spinning.

At any other time, Mist would have reveled in the time of day, the sun still high above the horizon, washing the sky with bold colors of red and yellow. She turned to her sister. "Tell me about Balder," Mist demanded, and the resolute set of her shoulders let her sister know that she would not be gainsaid.

Sighing, Astrid moved away from the open door, settling herself on a rock that overlooked the fjord. It was the very spot where she and Valdyr had had their conversation only last night. What was it about him that affected her so? Perhaps it was the desire to conquer what she saw in his eyes that in one way thrilled her, yet at the same repelled her. Whatever it was, she couldn't deny that the attraction was there. His very presence had set her senses to tingling in a way they never had before, as though they had suddenly taken on a life of their own. She had to pull her mind back from that memory to focus on what her sister was saying.

"I met him one day when I followed you to that spot." She glanced at Mist slyly. "I found the runes with the Christian cross. Whatever will *Far* have to say?"

Seeing the look on Mist's face, Astrid's eyes widened.

"Do not threaten me," Mist told her, the very timbre of her voice a warning.

Astrid flashed a repentant look. "I beg pardon, Mist. That was not my intent."

Mist allowed the falsehood to pass. "And what has that to do with Balder?"

"He was out that day exploring and stumbled upon me. We talked for a long time." She glared at Mist with frustrated defiance. "It was nice to be so admired."

Probably so. Mist could not say as she had never been the recipient of the kind of looks her sisters garnered.

"When we found that our farms were so near, we agreed to meet there again on that same day."

So they had met every *Tirsdag*. But for how long had it been going on?

Since her sister rarely stepped beyond the boundaries of their farm, she was surprised. Mist's irritation was a direct result of the fear that shook her. So much could have happened to her sister, especially so far from home. And she had her doubts as to whether Balder was exploring, or just searching for stray livestock that he could easily abscond with.

"And you told him that you will not see him again?" Mist asked.

Astrid nodded.

Mist smiled sadly at her sister's innocence. She doubted that Astrid knew the depths of obsession beauty like hers brought out in men.

"Does this have anything to do with Bjorn?" she asked.

The look that transformed Astrid's face told her that she had hit the mark. Her sister's blue eyes glowed more vividly than the morning sky.

"Truly, he should be called Bjorn *inn fagri*!" Astrid breathed softly.

Bjorn the handsome. Yes, Mist could certainly agree with that. They made an impressive couple.

A feeling of unease shivered through her, a dark premonition of impending doom that sent chills dancing along her nerve endings. Although he had retreated, she somehow doubted that Balder would give up so easily.

## Chapter 4

Mist watched from the open door as Valdyr left the farm after breaking the fast. He and his men had settled down into a regular routine on the farm. Each day they went searching for the white bear. It seemed the creature was moving in a more northerly direction, probably heading back to the water from whence it came.

Iceland was a very large island so searching was taking more time than expected. Little by little they were covering ground in their search, the signs becoming fresher and assuring them of a catch. If the animal did make it back to the water, it would probably disappear and the possibility of retrieving the valuable fur would disappear with it.

A part of her yearned to be in on the hunt, but that part of her was diminishing daily. It surprised her how much of a homebody she truly was. With Valdyr and his men here, she had been able to relax, and she found that she enjoyed helping Brita around the farm.

Mist had surprised Ari by joining him in milking the cows. It was hard, backbreaking work, but Mist was determined to quietly rebuild her strength.

At first, carrying the heavy buckets of milk they used for making cheese and butter had sent her to bed each night with arms and back aching. Now, the pain had lessened and she could see a change in her arms. Muscles that had once been like forged steel were once again taking on definition.

When no one was about, she would secretly take a sword and retreat to an area far from the farm so that she could not be seen. She refused to take the weapon to her favorite spot, feeling that it was sacrilege to desecrate the place with a weapon of war.

At first, it took everything she had just to lift the weapon, even though it was smaller and lighter than her normal sword. Now, after several weeks, she could once again jab, parry and thrust it. The whooshing sound of the sword as it cleaved the air started her blood singing in a familiar way. Her breathing deepened at the sense of power that once again surged through her.

"Impressive."

Startled, Mist turned, ready to strike.

Valdyr stood unmoved, the blade mere inches from his chest.

A frustrated growl emanated from Mist's throat at having been taken unawares. Only years of training had kept her from piercing the blade through Valdyr's body. She went cold at the image of him impaled and bloody. "I could have slain you!" she gritted between clenched teeth.

The small smile he gave her spoke his doubt, which only increased her ire and the longing to prove him wrong. It was so often a struggle to remember that she was now a child of the Christ. Taking a deep breath, she lowered the sword.

"What are you doing here?"

Valdyr lifted one eyebrow at her still surly tone. "I tracked the white bear this way." He allowed his gaze to slide over her before fixing once again on her eyes. "You should not be out here alone."

She clenched her teeth again. How was it that a man of his size and stature could move with such stealth? Surely his name fit him well, for he was as silent as a wolf, and she was very much afraid, just as dangerous. "And you should?"

He lifted the spear he held in his hand. "Hand-to-hand combat with a bear is not wise. A spear is a much better weapon of choice."

She knew that, but although she was gaining strength, throwing a spear with enough power to slay a white bear was still beyond her ability. Especially a spear the size of the one he carried. And if that didn't work, the ax tucked into his belt would surely bring down the largest animal. That was, if he threw it with accuracy, which she had no doubt he would.

He settled himself on a rock and studied her curiously, and she shifted uneasily. "How is it that you can face a thousand men fully armed for battle, and yet you scurry away like a fearful mouse whenever I come near you?"

Now how to explain that one! There was no way that she was about to feed his ego by letting him know that whenever he came around, her senses that warned her of imminent danger in battle came singingly alive.

"I do not scurry," she rebutted testily.

He got up off the rock and came toward her. Instinctively, she took a step in retreat until she saw his mocking smile, and then she firmly stood her ground, although it took every ounce of willpower she possessed. Her heart was thrumming at an alarming rate, matching the pulse she could see jumping in his throat.

She glared belligerently up into his face, despite the fact that, as tall as she was, she had to look a long way up to do so. This man would soon be her husband and yet he brought out in her the worst desire to be contrary. She felt it had something to do with the strength and power he emanated, making her feel weak in comparison.

Without saying a word, he slid a hand behind her neck, allowing his thumb to caress her lips. The icy-blue of his eyes was dwarfed under the expanding pupils until they were like shimmering onyx stones. Mist felt as though the very air around her had thickened and warmed.

He lowered his head toward her, and she felt a panicky need to flee, but another part of her kept her firmly rooted in place. Flee or stay? The decision was made for her when a voice called Valdyr's name.

He slowly allowed his hand to slide away and turned to face the intruder. Valdyr's face showed irritation at the interruption, but Mist offered up a thankful prayer for the timely intervention.

"Bjorn." Valdyr's voice was hardly encouraging. "What are you doing here?"

Bjorn glanced curiously from his brother to Mist. Seeing the sword in her hand, his eyebrows lifted upward in question.

"I saw you come this way and thought you might need a hand tracking the bear."

Mist saw her excuse to leave. "I must get back to the farm," she told them, brushing by Valdyr without looking up at him. She threw Bjorn a brief smile before she slipped the sword back into its baldric and made a hasty escape.

Valdyr watched her go with equal amounts irritation and admiration. He had looked into those shimmering green eyes and it was as though a lightning bolt from Thor's hammer had coursed through his entire body. His heart rate had yet to slow from their encounter. A cough from his brother only increased his irritation. He turned on him a look that in Bjorn's younger days would have subdued him. Bjorn only grinned.

"I take it that I interrupted something."

"You could say that," Valdyr replied.

"The question is," Bjorn continued, his tongue firmly in his cheek, "whether you were about to be decapitated, or whether you were about to steal a kiss."

Valdyr cocked a brow, letting him know in no uncertain terms that brothers were more a nuisance than a gift.

Bjorn chuckled, but then the humor fled his face. "Be careful, Brother. This Mist is not like other women."

Valdyr had come to that conclusion on his own. The more he was around her, the greater his desire to possess her. That the woman seemed reluctant only fueled that desire.

Bjorn changed the subject. "You saw signs that the bear came this way?" he asked.

Valdyr lifted a tuft of white fur that was clinging to a rock and handed it to his brother.

"He is heading for the ocean," Valdyr told him.

The thought of tracking the bear across the sea to some heretofore unknown land sent a thrill through Valdyr. The desire to be at sea instead of holed up as a farmer for a year left him gritting his teeth in frustration. The only thing that made the thought even close to palatable was knowing that at the end of that time, Mist would be his.

"Should we go after him?" Bjorn asked.

The feral gleam in his brother's eyes at the thought of the hunt matched the quickening of Valdyr's blood. He hefted his ax, giving his brother a grin.

"What are we waiting for?"

It took Mist the entire hour-long trek back to the farm to get her roiling emotions under control. Even then, if she thought about that look in Valdyr's eyes, her heart stalled and then started pounding all over again.

What would have happened if Bjorn hadn't interrupted? Would she have surrendered to this almost overwhelming desire to be the kind of woman she saw in Valdyr's eyes? It gave her an elemental feeling of power to know that a man finally found her not only attractive, but enticing, as well. It brought out the female in her that she had kept suppressed for so many years.

Too long she had denied herself and tried to be the son her father was lacking. Although the men of her acquaintance were impressed by her skill as a warrior, it was to women like Astrid that they turned when seeking a wife and companion. She had recognized early that many of them felt threatened by her. Not so Valdyr. She had the feeling that he saw her as a challenge, which just made her want to deny him that conquest. She didn't want to be conquered; she wanted to be loved, and she couldn't imagine Valdyr succumbing to such a weak emotion.

She entered the great hall and crossed to the far side of the building, where she hung her baldric on the peg made just for that purpose. She allowed her hand to slide over the sword and its case, memories of battles filling her mind. Although she had never slain just for the sport of it, like many of her people, she had been fiercely proud of the lives she had taken and survived to tell about it. After learning of God's love for mankind, guilt had weighed heavily on her, increasing immeasurably as she drew closer to the Christian God.

After Drustan had baptized her, she had been relieved of much of that burden, but she still felt guilt when she thought of all the men she had slain. She knew that God had forgiven her, but she was having a hard time forgiving herself.

So absorbed was she in her thoughts that when her sister Brita touched her on her shoulder, she nearly jumped from her skin. Startled at her response, Brita stepped back, one hand to her chest.

"Well, that is a first! I do not think that I have ever taken you unawares."

Mist frowned at her, irritated that her usually keen senses were so often clouded by her thoughts. "What is it you wish?" she asked testily.

Brita's eyebrows flew upward. "What ails you, Mist? You needn't be so sour," she remarked impatiently.

Instantly contrite, Mist gave a wry smile. There was no sense taking her frustration out on her sister. "I beg pardon, Brita. You are right."

Brita awaited an explanation that Mist was reluctant

to give. Ever since the arrival of Valdyr and his men, her whole world seemed suddenly topsy-turvy. Or had it started even earlier than that? If she gave it thought, she realized that she had felt out of place ever since giving her life to the Christian God. Nothing was the same, and yet, nothing was different. Except her.

Suddenly feeling the need to be alone, she told Brita again, "I beg pardon." Picking up her cloak where she had dropped it, she headed once more for the door.

"Mist!"

Ignoring her sister's demanding voice, Mist hurried outside. She glanced around to see if anyone, and by anyone she meant Valdyr, was about. Relieved to see no one except her kinsmen and servants doing their daily chores, she made haste to disappear before anyone could stop her. She ignored the twinge of guilt at abdicating her responsibilities to others, her restlessness driving her on.

She hadn't gone very far before she realized that she had done the very thing she had chastised her sister for; she had journeyed from the farm unarmed, except for her small dagger, which was strapped to her thigh and hidden beneath her tunic. She hesitated, but then chose to go forward. She needed time to think.

She found her favorite spot and settled on a rock, staring out at the mountains in the distance. There was a haziness to the air that she had never seen before. An eerie silence caused the hair on the back of her neck to rise. She got slowly to her feet, her tension increasing as she noticed the absence of birds in the vicinity.

The ground started to shake beneath her feet, intensifying until she had to cling to the rock outcropping to keep from falling.

It was not the first time she had felt the earth shake, but it had never been this strong and had never lasted this long. A loud explosion sounded, and in the distance a huge cloud of smoke billowed from the top of a distant mountain.

Mist stood mesmerized as pieces of the mountain shot high into the air. For an instant, she was terrified at the thought that the god Loki had burst his prison in the underworld to come and wreak havoc on this island of Iceland, but then she remembered that there was only one God, and that those she had learned of at her father's knee were mere myths. Or were they? If the gods of her people were mere vapors of mist, was the Christian God then angry at the people here for denying His Son? Was He about to destroy this island and all therein?

The plume of smoke rose high into the air, the winds taking it away from her and to the other side of the island.

How long she stood watching she had no idea, but the sun had already started its descent to the horizon. Against the darkening sky, the mountain could be seen in pinks and reds as it boiled from within.

She couldn't help but wonder if those who lived on the other side of the island were all right. Many of them were relatives.

Lifting her face to the sky, she began to pray the prayer that Drustan had made her memorize.

*Father in heaven, hallowed be Your name.*

Another explosion rocked the earth, throwing her to the ground. She remembered what the monk had taught her about the world being destroyed by fire. If this was the end, then she needed to be with her family.

Turning, she began to run back to the farm.

\* \* \*

Valdyr and Bjorn had just climbed to the peak of a rugged outcropping when the earth began to shake violently. Flailing his arms to keep his balance, Valdyr watched as his brother fell to the ground and rolled perilously near the steep edge of the cliff.

Throwing himself forward, he latched on to Bjorn's arm, pulling him away from the edge.

The shaking of the earth settled but was soon followed by a loud explosion and, in the distance, they could see what looked like the top of a mountain disintegrate and release a large plume of smoke into the air.

"Beard of Odin!" Bjorn exclaimed. "What is happening?"

Valdyr shook his head, his heart thundering in his chest. "I have no idea."

They both stood silently watching as the plume of smoke grew into a billowing mass and the ground began to shake again. From the top of the mountain, fiery liquid spewed forth, rolling down its sides and lighting up the deepening twilight.

"Could it be Ragnarok?" Bjorn asked in a breathless whisper.

The end of all things? Valdyr didn't believe that to be so. Surely when Ragnarok came, it would come with more fanfare than a spewing mountain and a little earth shake. No, this was something else entirely.

He had heard tales of this Iceland and its spewing mountains but had never given them much credence. Until now.

"Come," he told his brother. "We need to get back to the farm."

It was going to take them hours to get back, but a

voice inside compelled him to make haste. If Mist and her family were in any danger, he needed to be there. A surge of blood pumped through his veins in a fever tide and sent him scrambling back down the hill without thought of peril to his own life.

When they reached the bottom of the cliff, they began to run.

Covering the distance in ground-eating strides, they reached the farm only to find the compound in utter confusion.

Valdyr stopped, searching for any sign of Mist. When he saw her exit the house and run for the barn, he hurried after her, almost colliding with her when she came back out the barn door as he was about to enter. Grasping her by the shoulders, he scanned her shaking form for any sign of injury.

"Are you well?"

Her eyes were like huge green emeralds in her stark white face. He could see the fear in them that was running rampant through his own body. Wanting to ease that fear, he tugged her resisting form into his arms. She held herself aloof for mere seconds before finally surrendering. Clutching his shirt, she buried her face against his chest, and he could feel her slender form shaking uncontrollably. In those brief minutes that she allowed him to comfort her, the ice that had always surrounded his heart where women were concerned began to crack. The feel of her in his arms made him forget everything for the moment, including the exploding mountain, including their original antipathy toward each other.

She glanced up at him, and his eyes focused on her quivering lips. How was it that he had never noticed how red they were? Like the fruit of a ripe pomegranate.

He could tell the very instant she managed to tamp down her fear and assert her courage once again. Pushing out of his arms, she told him, "I have to see to the animals."

If she willingly allowed him to hold her once, there was the hope that she would do so again. Strangely, this gave him no superior feeling of conquest.

"I will help," he told her and followed her out the door, intent on keeping any harm from befalling her.

## Chapter 5

It had been three days since the earth shook, and still the mountain was emitting large volumes of smoke. When the wind shifted directions, the acrid scent moved in their direction, and ash settled lightly over their farm.

Brita grew aggravated with the extra amount of work this caused, and Mist couldn't blame her. Their washed clothes that had been hanging on the rope line outside had been covered in the dark matter and had to be re-washed, which was nearly impossible with ash still in the air.

Everyone, including animals, had been forced inside by the suffocating effects of the volcano. Mist was thankful for the large barns that her father had built, although the ground still shook periodically, and dirt from the thatch ceiling tumbled down onto them.

She took up the flat whalebone board and the black

onyx smoothing stone and began to press the wrinkles out of a shirt that Brita had washed earlier. It was a mindless task that Mist normally detested, but today, she welcomed being able to work.

The house was crowded with everyone being forced inside by the floating ash clouds. The animals were bellowing their discontent from the back reaches of the house.

The earth had shaken several more times since the first day, and Mist wondered if their island was about to be torn apart. The end had not come as she had first imagined. At least not so far. Hadn't Drustan told her that no man knew the hour, not even the Son? Voices lowered to whispers as everyone discussed what was happening. Some spoke of Loki, as she had at first believed. Still others spoke of Fenrir, the great wolf who would slay Odin when he finally broke the bonds of Gleipnir and began Ragnarok. Regardless of what anyone believed, it was an unsettling time, and Mist could almost smell the fear in the air. With each mention of the gods, she felt a twinge of disquiet inside herself. She wondered if it was because of the Spirit of God that Drustan had told her would come to live inside her, helping her to sense when she was outside God's will.

Her attention was suddenly caught by Valdyr talking about making a trek across the island, or sailing to the other side to see this billowing mountain up close. Mist thought him either moon touched or incredibly brave.

Erika came and sat next to her. "*Tante* Mist, I need to use the privy," she whispered urgently.

Mist glanced at her but her ear was straining to hear Valdyr's conversation. "Well, go then."

The child's face paled. "Will you go with me?"

The trembling words caught Mist's full attention. With all the talk of the wolf Fenrir breaking his chains, or the dark lord Loki breaking free from his forced prison, the child was terrified to go outside, and Mist could hardly blame her. She put aside her smoothing board and stone and pulled her niece up onto her lap. She wasn't sure how to reassure the child when she herself was so uncertain.

"You are afraid?" Mist asked her quietly, trying to avoid drawing attention.

Erika hesitated before nodding. Her eyes were round pools of blue in a stark white face.

"Being afraid is not something to be ashamed of," Mist reassured her, pushing tendrils of hair from the child's perspiring face. Despite the chill temperatures outside, with all of the extra bodies inside, the room was like a hot *sowna*.

"Are you afraid, *Tante* Mist?" she asked, her eyes like large moons.

Mist hugged her tightly. "Indeed I am, *elskling*. But do you remember me telling you about the one God and His Son?"

Erika nodded, a frown on her face as she tried to separate the stories her aunt had told from the things she was hearing now and had grown up with.

"Well," Mist told her, "when I am afraid, I pray to Him and He gives me peace. I know that He is with me no matter what happens or where I go."

"Even to the privy?" the child asked in horror.

Mist tried to keep from smiling. "Even there," she assured her. "Although I am certain that he grants me privacy."

Despite her skeptical look, Erika breathed out a sigh

of relief. "So if you go with me, He will come, as well?" she asked, beginning to squirm on Mist's lap. Mist decided that a full lesson on the Lord would have to wait for a more opportune time. Right now, her little niece was more concerned with making it to the outhouse before she had an accident.

Truth be told, Mist would be glad of a moment's reprieve from her forced imprisonment, the close confines only serving to make her more aware of the strange force that seemed to exist between her and her soon-to-be husband. When he had taken her in his arms, she had felt not only protected, but something she could not truly put a name to. She had been fully aware of his focused attention earlier this evening, but had forced herself to ignore him. It had been a relief when he had joined in a chess competition with the men earlier.

Mist set Erika off her lap and took her by the hand. At Brita's inquiring look, Mist motioned that they were going outside. Comprehending the necessity, her sister gave her a nod.

Erika hesitated at the door, but Mist squeezed her shaking hand. She was proud of her niece when she took a deep breath and plunged outside.

When they exited the house, they both stopped and stared in amazement. Even with the long darkness coming, it should not be this dark at this time of the day. The ash haze was so thick that it hid the sun from view. Mist shivered at the very eeriness of it.

Everything around her was covered in a layer of ash, even thicker than the snow that fell in the winter. Instead of a pristine world of bright white, the surrounding area was drab with gray and black, the scent of burning embers almost overwhelming.

Mist quickly pulled her apron up to cover her face. Erika began to cough as she inadvertently took in a lungful of the dusty specks.

"Cover your face, Erika," Mist warned. "And hurry!"

Erika wasted no time in the privy, but even in the short time Mist stood waiting for her, ash covered her hair and clothes, giving her the appearance of walking through a winter's blizzard. Except instead of melting on contact, the ash clung tenaciously to any surface it touched.

The two scurried back to the house as quickly as possible. When Mist opened the door, she plowed straight into Valdyr's solid chest, scattering ash in every direction. His firm grip on her upper arms kept her from tumbling backward onto the earthen floor. Those vivid blue eyes pushed every thought from her mind except that she could feel the heat from his body reach out and wrap around her. For what seemed an eternity they plumbed the depths of each other's eyes. She could only wonder what message she saw flashing there, but it was enough to muddle her thinking and start her heart pounding in her chest.

She finally managed to pull her gaze away, and he turned his attention to Erika. "Is everything well?" There was no disguising the concern in his voice.

The earthy scent of him teased at Mist's consciousness, bringing sudden fire to her cheeks. She pushed out of his hold, aggravated with both him and herself.

"Everything is well. Erika needed to make a trip outside."

"Ahh."

He smiled down in understanding at the child, and she grinned back at him. It was apparent that Erika had taken a liking to the hulking Norseman. The thought that she seemed to have, as well, Mist pushed aside to deal with later.

She bent to brush the ash off Erika's clothing and out of her hair, trying not to think about what she herself must look like. When she straightened, Valdyr proceeded to do the same for her, his touch once again bringing flaming color to her cheeks. Flustered, she moved out of his reach and proceeded to dust herself off. His knowing grin only served to reinforce her desire to keep out of his way. The man was simply too astute at reading her, something no man had ever done before.

"*Onkel* Valdyr, will you teach me to play *hnefatfl*?"

Erika had seen the men playing the game earlier as they tried to stave off the boredom of their forced imprisonment. It was much like the game of chess that most of them preferred, but took more concentration. Erika had begged to learn, but the men had impatiently pushed her away.

Mist opened her mouth to forestall Valdyr from hurting her niece's feelings, but she was shocked into instant silence when he bent to the child's level and bestowed on her one of his potent smiles.

"It would be my pleasure, *elskling*," he told her

Grinning from ear to ear, Erika scrambled across the room to find the *hnefatfl* board that Mist had brought her after a trip to Norway. Mist stood watching the child, trying to avoid Valdyr's look.

"That was very kind of you."

Valdyr shrugged his massive shoulders. "She is a sweet child."

Moving close again, he brushed at particles of ash that were still clinging to her hair, the gleam in his eyes reminding her of the wolf he was named after. Mist forced herself to remain still under his touch.

Valdyr was a true enigma. In all her years, she had never met a man like him. That same hand that could brandish a sword with deadly effectiveness was gently brushing ash from her hair in a way that made her heart react. How could the man stay so calm in the face of so much chaos?

Erika returned and took his attention. Mist was finally able to breathe, surprised that her hands were shaking. She watched the two cross the room and seat themselves on one of the earthen benches, and then went to join Brita, who was making the bread for the morrow. A moment of guilt flashed through Mist as she realized that she had done little of late to help her sister.

Mist took over Brita's job of turning the stone quern that would grind the barley seed into meal, thereby freeing Brita to begin joining yesterday's leaven with today's flour. She followed her sister's look to where Valdyr was patiently explaining the board game to her niece.

"I like him, Mist," Brita told her.

*As do I*, she thought, but refused to admit it out loud. She had the distinct feeling that if she brought her feelings out into the open, her life was going to change forever. One part of her responded to the man's magnetism, the other part feared it.

Brita glanced across the room to where Bjorn and Astrid were sitting close together, deep in some discussion. The two made a striking couple, but it was Bjorn's obvious love shining from his deep blue eyes that brought a smile to Mist's face.

"The women in our family have good taste in men. They will surely keep you warm on the long, dark nights,"

Brita stated, then burst out laughing as hot color flamed through Mist's cheeks.

Mist threw her sister a withering glare as Valdyr glanced their way, one brow lifted in inquiry. Mist promptly turned her back on him and began pounding the quern faster.

A fight broke out between some of the men, one accusing the other of cheating. Tempers had been escalating with each passing day of forced inactivity. A stern reprimand from Valdyr brought them under control, but Mist knew things were bound to get worse if something didn't change soon.

There were no further incidents that night, but when Mist finally lay down to sleep, she prayed that God would intervene in whatever darkness was spreading over the land. She yearned to feel the sun on her face and breathe in the fresh sea air from the fjord.

She tried to remember more of the words that Drustan had had her memorize, reassuring words that always brought calm. Instead, the only words that came to her mind were those she had overheard him mumbling one night when reading from his codex when he thought her asleep, words about darkness and gnashing of teeth.

Her family wasn't ready for judgment. She needed more time to try to reach them, to teach them about His Son and His holy word. If only she could remember more of those words that brought such consolation!

She lifted her face to the thatched ceiling above her and whispered a heartfelt prayer of only two words. *Lord, please.*

Then suddenly the words began to flow through her mind, those comforting words she had been searching for.

*My sheep hear My voice, and I know them, and they follow Me. And I give them eternal life; and they shall never perish, neither shall anyone pluck them out of My hand.*

Her body began to relax.

*He will never leave you nor forsake you.*

Her eyelids fluttered down, and she gradually fell into a peaceful sleep, her dreams of a man with sky-blue eyes.

When Mist awoke the next morning, she saw something she hadn't seen in several days. Sunlight poured in through the open door, lighting the house. She could tell that most of the people who had been entrenched inside were now gone.

Mist pushed away her bear pelt blanket and scrambled from her bed. She hurried over to the open door and looked outside, her eyes going wide at the sunshine bathing the landscape in the steadily decreasing light of winter.

Sometime during the night, the wind had shifted, blowing the remaining ash back to the other side of the island. Much of the ash that had fallen on their farm was gone.

She lifted her eyes to the sky and breathed a silent prayer of thanks. The budding faith that she clung to so tightly opened even further. She turned back inside and hurried to get dressed so that she could explore the farm for any damage that might have been done.

Brita was already busy preparing to break the fast. Mist stopped by her side, anxious to be outside but fully aware of her duty.

"Is there anything that I can do to help?"

Brita shook her head. "No. I can handle it." She gave Mist a knowing smile. "Go ahead."

Mist needed no further bidding. She ducked out the door and stopped to allow her eyes to adjust to the light.

As she wandered through the farm, she noticed heavy pockets of ash piled against objects that had stood in its way. Wherever ash had met water, it had congealed into a rock-hard mass.

Her aunt and the farming thralls were busy trying to recover the garden behind the storage buildings. They were raking back the ash to allow the sunlight to get to the vegetable plants. Other thralls were taking the cattle out to pasture farther inland, their first time out in days, as well.

Mist remembered Valdyr talking about taking the ship to the other side of the island and quickly made her way to the harbor.

Valdyr and his men were busy on the longship, unloading the oars, shields that hung on the side and the wool sail. After emptying the boat, they used shoveling tools to dig out the ash and throw it over the side.

Her father was standing next to Valdyr, watching the work. Mist made her way to them, noting their grim faces.

When Valdyr turned those ice-blue eyes on her, she felt that familiar tingle along her body, all the way to her toes.

"Do you still plan on making a trip to see the fire mountain?" she asked.

He nodded. "Your father is concerned about the welfare of those living close to it."

She nodded. The same thought had occurred to her.

Many in the vicinity were friends, some distant relatives. "I would like to go with you."

He was already shaking his head before the words made it from her mouth. She gave a sigh of frustration. Her father glanced from Valdyr's set face to Mist's equally determined expression.

"We need your help here on the farm," her father told her, trying to stave off confrontation.

She glared at Valdyr. He wasn't her husband yet, so why did he think he had any say over her actions?

"Brita has enough help. I need to see what damage has been done, and if there is anything we can do to be of assistance."

Valdyr threw back his head, folded his arms across his chest and glared right back. If he hoped to turn her into a quivering mass of jelly he was doomed to disappointment. The only time those blue eyes had any such effect on her was when the look in them made her flatteringly aware that she was a woman.

"Mist is right," her father said surprisingly. "She knows every nook and cranny on this island. She would be a great help to you."

Something in Valdyr's expression made Mist pause. "The trip will take some time as I intend to explore the island, and there will be little privacy on the open sea," he said.

Before her conversion, she wouldn't have given it a second thought, but she remembered Drustan's words about men's desires and a woman's responsibility to act and dress modestly. The gleam in Valdyr's eyes did nothing to relieve her hesitation, but her pride made her push such thoughts aside. She wouldn't have the men believe that she was some weak woman they could take advantage of.

"I will make do," she told him.

Their warring gazes clashed like steel swords. Valdyr said nothing for a long moment. Breathing in a frustrated breath, he said, "As you wish. We will be leaving within the hour."

Mist nodded. "I will gather some supplies."

She could feel Valdyr's penetrating eyes on her back as she retreated. When her father had sided with her, she had felt a childish desire to stick out her tongue at her intended husband. The temptation to look over her shoulder and do so now was strong, but she ignored it.

Valdyr watched her walk away, pushing down the irritation he felt. It had taken no imagination to read the look in her eyes. It plainly let him know that he was not her husband yet. Well and good, but when he was, things were certainly going to change.

At Bjorn's call, he pulled his gaze from Mist and made his way to the ship to help with the cleanup. He met Egil's amused look before the older man turned and followed his daughter. It was easy to see where the woman got her irritating ways.

They were almost finished when Mist returned with several thralls carrying large baskets of supplies.

Valdyr slowly rose from his kneeling position where he was brushing the ash from the overlapping planks on the outside of the ship. He looked at Mist in astonishment.

"I had not intended to stay very long," he told her.

She motioned to the thralls to load the baskets onto the ship. "It is better to be safe than sorry."

Valdyr studied her in narrow-eyed appraisal. What on earth was the woman thinking? The ship would be cramped enough as it was with him taking all twenty of his men to more speedily row to the other side of the island and back again. Winter was fast approaching. "Surely you cannot believe that my men are that ravenous," he mocked.

He was brought up short by something curious in her expression. He frowned, glancing from Mist to the loaded baskets.

"The supplies are not for us, are they?" he asked suspiciously. His guess was proven correct when several other thralls followed from the house, also loaded down with baskets of food.

Valdyr hesitated, knowing that the suffocating ash was going to wreak havoc on their own gardens. Much of the area was still covered by ash that had mixed with moisture and become very like the Romans' cement. He was having a hard enough time scraping it from the hull of the ship. If they didn't get it removed, it would weigh the ship down and clog the air passages between the planking that allowed for swift movement. There was no telling what damage had been done to their crops.

At the same time, there were probably others in much worse condition. He should have thought of that. On such an isolated, inhospitable island, it would be prudent to be of assistance.

He glanced back at Mist. "Do you need any help?"

Seeing that he understood what she was about, she smiled. "I was about to ask you the same thing."

He bent to the task at hand, more to avoid looking at Mist than because there was much left to do.

"We are almost ready to leave," he told her. "Would you let your father know?"

As she turned to leave, the breeze she stirred wafted her scent to him, a curious mixture of the fresh outdoors, the scent of baking bread and the woman she was. Breathing deeply, it affected him in ways he was unprepared for. His mental image of her as a shield maiden was replaced by a picture of her lovingly tending her niece, who then in his mind became a babe; his babe.

His breathing hitched momentarily. Strong attraction was tempered with an even stronger desire to protect her from anything and anyone, including himself. Now wasn't that just a fine kettle of fish.

## Chapter 6

They set out much later than Valdyr had anticipated, so he decided to go with the current that flowed westerly around the island instead of rowing against it and shortening the distance. It would also give him an opportunity to see more of this island of ice and fire.

He glanced at Mist sitting in the center of the boat, her eyes closed, her face lifted to the cool ocean breeze as the sail caught the wind and they plowed along, the longboat skimming through the water with ease. The sunlight reflected off her vivid red hair, giving it shimmering gold highlights. His breath caught in his throat at the picture she made. Her attractiveness was steadily growing on him and his fascination with her was mounting daily regardless. It was going to be a long winter if he had to be holed up at the farm during the cold months, watching her day in and day out, yet wait until autumn to make her his wife.

The dread he had felt sailing here had long ago been replaced with anticipation that had crept up on him unaware. He had always been a man who liked a challenge, and Mist had been a challenge from the start. He was having a hard time deciding if it was his desire to conquer that was plaguing him, or an actual interest in the woman.

Motion off to his left took his attention. A whale suddenly breached the surface, its black-and-white body arcing gracefully into the air before slamming back into the sea, shooting a spray of water high into the sky. A familiar thrill coursed through Valdyr as he watched the whale disappear below the surface once again.

The ripples from the breaching whale shook their ship as they plowed through water, the strong currents and ocean breeze making quick work of the distance they were traveling.

His men glanced at him in expectation, their excitement evident. He hesitated, the desire to hunt surging through him, but then he shook his head and the men settled back into a brooding silence. He could well understand their disappointment. After several weeks of farming life, the longing for the excitement of a hunt was growing strong among them all. Unlike their brethren, they were seafaring men who followed the strong pull of adventure. Lately, though, he found his own desires being pulled in a much different direction, particularly toward the woman in his ship.

He noticed that Mist's attention had been arrested by the whale, as well. She continued to search the rippling water, obviously hoping for another sighting. Her patience was rewarded minutes later as the whale surfaced again, its path taking it away from them on its winter migration route.

He took a seat near her. His heart rocked quite heavily when she turned on him those glowing green eyes sparkling now with her pleasure at having seen such a marvelous sight.

"They never cease to amaze me," she said, her breathy voice increasing his heart rate to match the swift rowing of the oars.

Vexed by his physical reaction to such a paltry thing, he gave her a halfhearted smile. "Nor me. It pains me when I have to slay one." Killer whales were fierce predators, free and wild, and he felt a certain kinship with them in his spirit. They didn't go quietly in battle, and often the hunter became the hunted.

Her return smile was full of understanding. Although farmers, their people's livelihoods were heavily dependent on the sea and everything in it. It was a greater source of nourishment during the long, dark winters. A single whale could feed a colony for much of the winter. Perhaps he should have given more consideration to the chase, but he was more intent on reaching the fire mountain, and he was also concerned about Mist's safety. Whales had been known to sink a longship. There would be time enough for hunting later.

They sailed always within sight of Iceland's shores, but the spewing mountain disappeared as they rounded the southwest side of the island. Here, everything looked normal. The windblown ash hadn't reached here. They passed peaceful farms nestled into the rocky hillsides, their tenants going about their daily business, stopping to stare at the passing ship. Regardless of imminent threats, life had to go on.

The land on this side of the island was impressive. The farms were widespread, and Valdyr could see that come summer, the area would be richly green. Egil's farm was good, but these were excellent. This is where the first settlers landed and took the choicest locations.

Valdyr took the opportunity to study the areas as they sailed along. He was impressed with the amount of fish in these waters, including whales, seals and dolphins. Where larger fish congregated there would have to be a source of smaller fish for them to survive, and those smaller fish would sustain his people, as well. The stockfish here had turned into a great source of trade, the wind-dried cod was easy to transport. The *skreid* was extremely popular back on the mainland.

When they landed each evening he made treks inland to scout out the land and its occupants. Very little wildlife surfaced on the rocky island, but he caught sight of the white foxes and numerous kinds of birds. By the time they had almost reached their destination, Valdyr had concluded that the white bear they had been hunting had not been indigenous to the island. No others had been spotted, and he had yet to see a sign of the one they had been tracking.

After they rounded the northernmost portion of the island, the more apparent the signs of the erupting volcano. Melting ice from the surrounding vicinity had made the rivers rise, their fast-flowing waters rushing across the beaches and emptying into the sea, taking debris with them, including several dead sheep.

Valdyr stared at the chaos grimly. Had the people here escaped with their lives, or were they buried beneath that hardening lava?

Mist picked her way among the men and came to

stand carefully beside him in the prow. He glanced down and noticed the look of sympathy on her face.

He shook his head. "It does not look good."

The loss of life was bad enough, but land was at a premium here, and this portion had just been rendered uninhabitable.

More ash had settled here than on their farm, thanks to the prevailing winds. Farms here had quickly been abandoned as they were swallowed up by the hot river of lava. The still-smoking rocks warned them to keep far away. Frowning, he turned to Mist.

"Where would the people go?"

She nodded her head toward the interior. "Farther inland. Most of the land around the edges of the island has been claimed, at least that which could be farmed."

When they reached a place where they could finally land, they pulled into shore. Leaving some men to protect the ship, he took the rest, and with Mist along, headed for the interior and the still-flowing mountain. Warriors his men might be, but he had to bite back a grin at the obvious relief of those staying behind. They feared nothing they could actually face in battle; it was the unknown that unsettled them. As for him, he had never really believed in all the stories told to him as a child about the gods his people worshipped and feared. He wasn't certain what he believed, or if he believed in anything. Still, the eeriness of burning pillars rising from the depths of the smoky landscape set his teeth on edge.

He glanced at Mist and took note of her serene countenance. When others were worried and fretful, she always seemed so at peace. He had noticed that others tended to gravitate to her without even realizing it. She was like the magnetic stones that attracted objects to them without any effort of their own.

Even now, the thought that they could possibly all be slain didn't seem to faze her. Was she like this when she marched into battle, or was this a result of a conversion to the Christian God? It was getting harder to imagine her as a shield maiden fighting on the battlefield. Where before he could picture her green eyes blazing, red hair flowing about her in a fiery wave, her sword flashing in the sunlight as it cleaved its way through the enemy, now that picture was replaced by her calmly tending a home and children. He wasn't certain which attracted him most.

He shook his head in irritation. He was becoming maudlin in his aging years.

Mist followed behind Valdyr, carefully stepping in his tracks through the fine layer of ash that had settled even this far from the area most affected. They had quickly realized that hidden dangers lay beneath the depth of the ashes. Tripping over hidden rocks was bad enough, but what had seemed solid ground had one time turned out to be a cleft in the ground that, filled with the light ash, caused one of Valdyr's men to sink into a hole up to his neck. Moss-covered stones peeked like a small army of green gnomes out of the ash-blanketed hills.

The closer they got to the mountain, the more foul smelling the air became, much like eggs that had been rotting for a long time. Wrinkling her nose, Mist covered her mouth and nose with her shawl until the wind would shift and push the scent away once again.

By the time they clearly sighted the mountain in the distance, its rocky surface looming upward out of a haze of smoke, Mist was about to drop with exhaustion. Nights trying to sleep in the longship had left her tired and out of sorts, but after miles of walking over the rough ground, she was just about ready to admit that she shouldn't have come. It irritated her that Valdyr seemed to suffer no such effects. Did the man never get tired?

They stopped to make camp as the sun was beginning its descent. Although there would be dim light left as the sun moved closer to the earth, since it never truly set they would still be able to see for miles, though their visibility would be limited and thus dangerous in such conditions. Whatever their reasons for stopping, Mist let out a protracted sigh of thankfulness.

They set up their camp using the brush they had been able to scrounge together to make a fire. Mist handed out to the men the bread she had brought with her and then collapsed near the fire. Valdyr seated himself next to her on the hard ground and offered her some dried seal meat. She wasn't particularly fond of the tough and chewy meat, but it was best for use in long trips. She took the meat and thanked him, settling back to watch the shimmering colors of light that began to fill the darkening sky.

Ever since the volcano had erupted, the lights had taken on a greater brilliance of orange, red, green and purple, and it was a joy just to watch them shift and swirl across the nighttime expanse. It was hard to see them as some ominous portender of doom when they were so incredibly beautiful.

Valdyr's voice interrupted her contemplation.

"I suppose you believe that your Christian God is responsible for all of this?" he asked, motioning with his hand to include both the undulating sky lights and the mountain in the distance now glowing red-orange in the deep twilight.

She answered with a question of her own. "I suppose you believe that a quarreling multitude of gods did?"

He gave her an enigmatic look. "I don't believe in anything but what I can see, taste or feel."

A thoughtful smile turned up her lips. "Even the simplest minds know that something can't exist without having first been created, and yours is no simple mind."

At his look of surprise, she wondered what had made her say such a thing. He frowned.

"And what of the other gods we have encountered in our years? What makes you think that this Christian God is the right one?"

How could she explain?

"My sisters and I have our differences of opinion, but we always manage to work things out peacefully."

His frown deepened. "What has that to do with the Christian God?"

She turned from studying the sky to watching his face in the deepening darkness. Keeping her voice low so as not to disturb the others, she told him, "My father loves us all. Although Brita and I know that he favors Astrid more, he never takes sides in our arguments. But we have no doubt that he would step in if things became physical."

One blond brow winged its way upward. "Are you equating your father with this god, then?"

She smiled slightly, pleased that he was following along with what she was trying to say while not totally understanding.

"Only in the fact that God, the true God, loves all of His children. The fact that some have been swayed to other beliefs is not His fault. From the beginning of time, God has made His presence known—first, through the world He has created, and finally through His written word. His children make war amongst themselves, but He does not step in and take over to bring them to Him. Each one is certain that their way is right. God has given us free will to make that choice on our own. In His written word it tells us that God does not show favoritism."

"Unlike Odin or Thor."

Mist nodded her head in agreement, watching his face. The glow from the crackling fire added bright planes and dark shadows to his features, the reflected light in his eyes making them glow with an almost unearthly sheen.

"I think I understand what you are saying, but it still does not explain how you know that this Christian religion is the right one."

She was frustrated that she didn't have the words to make him understand. And why was he suddenly so interested? Was he beginning to doubt his choice of wife?

"It is hard to explain the feelings that you experience when you accept the sacrifice of the Christ and know that the relationship between you and God, the Father, has been restored."

It was also hard to explain the up and down emotions when struggling to follow the way of the Lord despite what she had always been taught. She believed in the Christian God, yet she struggled daily. Would she ever be as clear in her beliefs as Drustan?

Valdyr let out a deep sigh and turned to watch the bubbling cauldron in the distance. The lengthening silence grew uncomfortable, and Mist shifted nervously as she watched him from under lowered lashes. What was the man thinking that had turned his face to stone? Did he sense her own doubts and insecurities?

"Get some sleep," he told her, the curious inflection in his voice making her frown.

Every time she thought they were growing closer to an understanding, something seemed to drive them apart. She couldn't help but wonder if it was the Christian God. Well, she could remember Drustan's admonition not to align herself with an unbeliever. *For what has light to do with darkness?* The words echoed around in her mind like the sound that echoed back at her from the surrounding mountains. But what about obedience to her father?

Crawling into the tent that Valdyr had erected for her, Mist pulled the bear pelt over her shivering form and settled close to the opening where the fire still burned. Tiredness overwhelmed her. In the moment before she dropped into a deep sleep, drifting in a world of semi-wakefulness, she felt a featherlight brush across her forehead that warmed her more thoroughly than the crackling fire.

## Chapter 7

Mist slowly awakened to loud voices in the semidarkness. The sun was still hours away from full daylight. Valdyr must have decided to leave early.

Giving a soft groan, she groggily pushed herself up to a sitting position and rubbed the sleep out of her eyes, stifling a desire to sleep longer. The cold quickly wrapped her in its chilling arms when she pushed off the bear pelt. Shivering, she pulled her white fox cape from the stack of bedding and wrapped it around her shoulders. Every bone in her body ached from lying on the cold, hard ground, despite the pelts she had used for her bed.

Stretching like an Egyptian cat, she wondered what Valdyr was arguing with the men about, and who would have the audacity to disagree with him in the first place.

A vaguely familiar voice separated itself from the others and brought her to instant wakefulness. She blinked her eyes, trying to see the man who was now speaking to Valdyr.

The man stepped closer to the light of the dwindling fire, and Mist caught her breath. She scrambled hastily to her feet, any ideas of further sleep totally forgotten. Pushing out of the tent, she stumbled forward.

"Lord Finn!"

Finn's family owned one of the farms on the far side of the island, the side that had been devastated by the volcano. Although he was not blood family, it was good to see him alive and well.

He turned to her, the frown on his face transforming instantly into a broad smile. Although near her father in age, Finn was still lean and muscled. One eye was covered by a patch from a battle that had left him with a scar that ran down the length of his face. His gaze settled on her, bringing back memories she had been trying hard to forget.

He was a keen leader in battle, his fierce look bolstering courage in a wavering heart. He had done that for her when her arms had grown weak and the battle had seemed lost; she had a great respect for him and that reverence had rung forth when she called his name.

"Mist! I did not expect to see you here!"

The delight in his voice was unmistakable. Valdyr glanced suspiciously from one to the other, and Mist hastened to explain.

"Lord Finn fought with us in the battle at Hafrsfjord," she told him, joining them by the fire.

Finn's face turned serious. "I heard about your fall," he commiserated, frost rings forming in the cold morning air when he spoke.

"Odin must have favored you to allow you to return to the land of the living."

Several warriors were standing behind Finn, including his son, Knut, who was glowering at her, his handsome bearded face marred by a longstanding hate. She had dented his pride by besting him once in a sword fighting contest, and he had never forgotten, nor forgiven, her.

"More than likely Odin's Valkyries refused to take her to Valhalla," he sneered, and several of the men chuckled at his wit.

Mist settled a glare on each of the smirking men. "It was not Odin who saved me, but a monk from Eire who serves the one true God."

There was instant silence at this pronouncement followed by a discontented murmuring from the men behind Knut.

"It is likely *her* fault that the gods are against us. She has embraced that heathen religion of the English," Knut announced. The murmuring increased, and seeing that he had received a favorable response, he continued, "We should take her to the top of the mountain and throw her in. Mayhap the gods would then be appeased."

Before Mist could answer him, Valdyr stepped between them, his hand resting on his broadsword. His quiet voice rumbled with lethal intent. "Mayhap you would like to try."

If Mist could best Knut in a sword fight, she had no doubt of the outcome should he test Valdyr in such a way. Knut must have been thinking much the same thing. Some of the bravado left his face at Valdyr's fierce countenance.

The men behind Knut reached for their swords, as did Valdyr's men.

"Hold!" Finn commanded, glancing from Knut to Valdyr, recognizing the threat to his son. "Be silent, Knut," he commanded, his fierce expression causing his own men to slowly sheath their weapons. He turned to Mist. "I beg pardon for my son, Mist. His mouth often works faster than his head."

Mist fought to keep from making some scathing statement of agreement. Knut had always been a bully, and she doubted he would ever change. His pride was one day going to be his undoing.

She pushed aside the voice inside her head reminding her that she had been very like him not so long ago and turned her attention to the older man.

"Why are you here, Finn?"

He blew out a frustrated breath. "Our farm was hit by the lava. It moved so fast that we didn't have time to do more than grab what we could and run. I fear all of our livestock is lost. But more than that, my youngest son was herding the sheep near the mountain when it erupted." His voice lowered until Mist had to strain to hear it. "I fear he is lost, as well."

As the sunlight increased, Mist could now make out a larger group of people standing farther away. She recognized Finn's wife, her face wreathed in anguish, standing next to a younger woman, who was carrying a babe. Their long kirtles were almost black from ash, their *hustrinet* headwear, as well.

"We were able to take few supplies with us so we have been searching out game, of which there is very little. If we cannot find something soon…"

He left the words unsaid, and Mist laid a hand on his

arm in sympathy. She turned to Valdyr, only to find that his attention was still on Knut. "We have brought supplies, Finn. They are in Valdyr's ship that is in the fjord that joins this river." At his look of appreciation, she warned him, "The supplies will not last long. If there are others in the same fix, we will need to share with them, as well."

He nodded in agreement. "I understand. At least it will give us a little more time to decide what to do."

"Where will you go?" Valdyr asked, finally releasing Knut from his stare.

"Farther inland. The land there is not as favorable for farming, but it will have to do. It will just mean working a little harder."

"Not for me," Knut disagreed. "I intend to go back to Norway and leave this desolate place."

His father glared at him. "And where will you go? The land there is already taken. There is nothing for you there."

The young woman who had been standing near Finn's wife came forward still clutching the baby. She smiled hesitantly at Knut. "And how will we get there, my husband?"

He glared down at her. "*I* have already made plans. *You* will stay here with my father."

Her face whitened at his angry voice, and she hurriedly stepped away. Finn placed a consoling hand on her shoulder. "It is all right, Iliana. We will discuss this later."

Knut looked as if he was about to argue but the look on his father's face made him hesitate. Nostrils flaring, he pressed his lips tightly together and stomped away in the direction of the fjord. The others, one by one, slowly began to follow after him, except Finn.

Mist glanced at Iliana sympathetically as she passed. Having such a husband, the woman needed all the prayers that she could get, and since Mist was the only one in the vicinity who had even a hint of a relationship with God, she decided then and there to add Iliana to her daily prayers.

"We are grateful for your assistance," Finn told Valdyr. Respect bloomed in Valdyr's eyes, and he nodded his acceptance of the older man's gratitude. He watched as Finn turned and followed after his people. Valdyr glanced down at Mist.

"Let us go, as well. I no longer have a desire to see inside the mountain."

Relieved, Mist followed him back to the ship. As she walked along, she lifted up praise to God for keeping her family safe, as well as asking mercy for Lord Finn and his clan. Although Knut had belittled her faith, Lord Finn had looked at her with a wealth of respect, giving her hope that she might be able to someday reach some of her people with the saving truth of Christ.

Valdyr kept watch on the one called Knut. He hadn't missed the enmity for Mist radiating from the young man's eyes. What had she done to incite such a reaction? The only thing that came to mind was that she had at one time rejected his suit.

The woman of his thoughts was striding along at his side, deep in thought, as well. If the mountain were to explode again, he doubted it would catch her attention. What was on her mind that had her so absorbed?

She hurried forward to catch up to Finn's wife and

daughter-in-law. He couldn't hear their words, but the other two women smiled, and Iliana placed her child in Mist's reaching arms. There was such a look of longing on Mist's face as she smiled down at the babe that Valdyr felt his breath catch at the sight. The woman would make a wonderful mother, unlike his own, who had divorced his father when Bjorn was just a child. With each passing day he became more certain that he and Mist would have a good life together, and he was becoming more impatient to begin that life.

Egil had told him that she had agreed to the marriage only on the condition that she would be given time to get to know her future husband, and she was steadfast in her determination not to enter into that contract before the autumn harvest. He wanted to think of a way to make her change her mind. Mayhap he could work on her father, instead.

It had taken them hours to trek inland, and now it would take even longer to return to the ship traveling with Finn's weary band.

Whenever they stopped to rest, Mist would return the child to its mother and Mist and Iliana would sit with their heads close together. What they found to talk about, Valdyr had no idea, but it was apparent they had formed a bond of friendship in the short time they had been together. He realized that he had never seen Mist laugh with such abandon. Just the sound of it lightened his heart and brought a smile to his face.

The sun was beginning to set in vivid shades of orange and red when they finally reached the peaceful fjord where his ship was resting on the cold blue water. His men, however, having seen the throng of people headed their way, were fully armed and ready for battle, their iron swords gleaming in the waning sun.

Valdyr shoved his way to the head of the band to forestall any aggression on his men's part and to assure them of their safety. When they saw him, they lowered their swords ever so slowly, ready to raise them at his command.

Seeing the ship and knowing that supplies were waiting, Finn's band began to push onward only to stop as those guarding the ship raised their swords threateningly once more.

"Peace, Amund," he called to his second in command, and the other man turned from studying the group to Valdyr himself. Amund's bearded face gave away nothing of his thoughts and feelings. Broad muscles that had been tensed for battle slowly eased.

Finn joined Valdyr beside the ship. "What do you need us to do?" he asked.

Busy searching out Mist's location, he barely heard the man. He finally spotted her holding Iliana's child, Iliana and Finn's wife by her side. Knut stood farther away with a group of men.

Satisfied that Knut was nowhere near Mist, Valdyr turned back to Finn and said, "Why don't your men help us unload some of the supplies and then we will help you set up camp for the night."

Finn rattled off commands to his people and after several moments of confusion, they were organized into various groups, some to make a fire, others to set up sleeping arrangements and still others to parcel out the food.

When everything was finally situated to Finn's satisfaction, Mist approached him, and Valdyr tensed, still uncertain of the man's relationship to her. He hadn't missed the wealth of feeling in her greeting to the older man.

"Lord Finn, your family is welcome to come to my father's farm for shelter. Winter is fast approaching and you will not have time to set up your home."

Finn shook his head. "No, Mist, but I thank you. There will be others in the same situation, looking for new land to settle and there is precious little of that left. We need to find someplace of our own."

Valdyr could well understand his reasoning. It would not go well with such a leader to become someone else's chattel, and that is what it would seem if he had to be someone's tenant farmer. He watched the other man struggle with whatever he wanted to say. Finn finally continued.

"I would send my wife, daughter and grandchild with you."

"No!"

Finn's wife hurried to his side. "I will not go without you. Where you go, I will go."

"You will do as I say, Edda."

Although the words were harsh, the look in Finn's eyes as he stared down at his wife was in direct contrast. She looked as though she was about to argue, but then pressed her lips together and remained silent. Without any words, the two carried on a conversation that only they could understand. Valdyr envied them that closeness. Did it come from years of being together, or was it a result of the love they so obviously shared? He scoffed inwardly. Since when had he started giving such consideration to that particular emotion? He glanced across at Mist and realized that he had his answer.

Edda finally gave a sigh of capitulation and returned to Iliana's side.

Finn turned back to Valdyr. "I will take some of my men with me, and send the others on the horse path with the women and children to Egil's farm. They should reach the farm about a week after you."

The horse paths were worn paths that traversed the island, allowing for faster travel. It was a wise decision to use them.

"Perhaps I should send half of my men with your men, as well. That way we could take the women and children in the boat."

Finn shook his head. "No. It would be better for you to return as quickly as possible to apprise Lord Egil of our imminent arrival."

That was probably true. With his cattle and sheep disappearing, Egil was on edge and might possibly see such a large group of men as a threat, especially if he didn't recognize Valdyr's men among them.

"As you wish," Valdyr agreed.

Knut stepped to his father's side. "I will go with the women and children."

"No. You will not," Valdyr disagreed, pulling himself up to his full height. His hostile look met Knut's, and it took an iron will to keep from knocking the insolent look from the younger man's face. There was no way that he was going to allow this man anywhere near Mist.

Finn glanced at Valdyr's set face. "I agree. I will need you to help me set up the land."

Knut glared at both men. "I wish to be with my wife and child."

"Then perhaps you wish them to remain here with

you," Valdyr suggested coldly, folding his arms across his chest, his narrow eyes daring Knut to challenge him.

"No," Finn answered quickly. "That is not necessary. We will rejoin them later, after we have claimed our land."

Knut's rapid breathing spoke of feelings longing to spew forth. Then he turned and strode off. Valdyr noticed that despite what he had said earlier, he joined his men instead of his wife and child.

Valdyr felt sorry for Iliana as she seemed to be a nice sort. But truth to tell, he really wouldn't mind making the woman a widow, and if Knut continued to watch Mist with that look of pure hatred, he would more than likely make it so sooner rather than later.

Appetites finally replete, everyone settled down for the night in small groups, several fires dotting the darkening landscape to ward off the approaching chill. In the distance, the mountain still glowed red but it was no longer the billowing black mass of before.

Valdyr seated himself next to where Mist was adding kindling to the fire. She had finally given back Iliana's baby, but reluctantly. Now she stared mesmerized by the dancing firelight.

"You are quiet tonight," he told her.

One side of her mouth turned up wryly. "You make it sound as though I am normally a chattering jay."

Valdyr blew out a scoffing breath. "That can certainly not be said of you."

She grinned at him, but said nothing. He waited patiently, hoping that she would share whatever was worrying her. If she was concerned about Knut, she needn't be. He would protect her with his life, as would any of his men. In the weeks they had come to know her, she had impressed them all; not only with her skill as a swordsman, but with the kind way she had treated everyone.

She glanced over at Finn, and he saw her eyes soften to a glowing emerald. Jealousy twisted through him, surprising him with its intensity. Could she be enamored of the older man?

"I am concerned for Lord Finn and his family. The weather here is so unpredictable. And he is a proud man. He will not take kindly to owing any man."

She threw a stick on the now glowing embers. Sparks flew up into the air, lighting her face briefly.

Valdyr followed her look to the man and saw what she was seeing. Despite Finn's robust physical appearance, his age was telling on him. His shoulders drooped with concern over his family.

Valdyr glanced back at Mist. "You have strong feelings for the man."

It was more a question than a statement and demanded an answer. Her eyes widened at the tone of his voice.

"I owe him my life," she told him, and he waited for her to continue. "Before we went to Hafrsfjord, we fought together at Leuven. We were sorely outnumbered, but we made up for our lack of numbers with sheer determination." She paused, a faraway look coming to her eyes. As she described the battle, he could picture it in his own mind having been in the same situation many times himself. He wondered if his own eyes reflected the same kind of anguish he now saw in hers when he recounted his battles for others.

"You do not have the heart of a warrior," he stated quietly, wondering how she had endured such things as she must have experienced. "You are far too soft."

Her eyes flashed with enough fire to rival the crackling embers that lit up her angry face. "When it comes
to defending my family and my way of life, I can be as
fierce as any other warrior," she disagreed vehemently.
But as quickly as her anger had flared, it disappeared.
"You are right, in one way. When it comes to pillaging
and plundering, burning and slaying just for the sport
of it, it makes me ill to even think of such things." Eyes
dark with images only she could see, she told him, "With
every life I took I thought about him being someone's
son. Or husband. Or father," she finished huskily.

How did this woman ever survive even her first
battle?

"Like your brother-in-law?"

She said nothing, merely looking at him with those
sad eyes full of remembered pain.

He looked out over the group of people in various
stages of retiring for the night and caught Knut once
again glaring at Mist. He felt his own rage begin to
churn through him.

"Why does Knut hate you so much?" he asked Mist.

Mist glanced at Knut. Seeing her attention suddenly
fixed on him, Knut turned away, quickly looking elsewhere.

Mist sighed. "I bested him once in a sword fighting
contest."

Valdyr could certainly understand the embarrassment of being bested by a woman, but he sensed that
Knut's hatred went much deeper than that. Whatever
had caused it, Valdyr knew that he would have to keep
a closer watch on the two.

"You need not concern yourself overmuch," she told

him, seeing his fierce glare at the other man. "Where Knut is concerned, I can take care of myself."

"Perhaps," he agreed. "But know this. As long as I am around, you will not have to."

Instead of the hostility he expected, she smiled her appreciation. He returned her smile. He had the feeling that in this emotional game of chess, he had finally managed, for the first time, to put her into check.

## Chapter 8

A thick fog had sprung up during the night and lay heavy over the land. Disembodied figures moved in and out of sight through the mist as the crew loaded the ship for departure. Voices echoed off the soupy air as mothers called to their children and Finn's people readied themselves for the long trip across the island.

Mist sat on the cold ground beside Edda as they waited for the fog to lift. It would be foolhardy to travel in such murky weather. That was one thing about this island of ice and fire; the weather could change in an instant.

Edda was watching her daughter-in-law as Iliana took leave of her husband. Mist had felt an instant affinity for them both, and was glad that they would be coming to Egilsfjord.

Knut's face never softened as he talked with Iliana. Whatever he said made the color flee from her face. She dropped her eyes to the ground in what Mist considered to be a subservient manner that should be restricted to servants, not wives. Her tense shoulders gave a clear indication that she didn't like what was being demanded of her.

Frowning, Edda shook her head regretfully. Tucking a straggling gry wisp of hair behind her *hustrinet* head scarf she told Mist, "Knut could not ask for a finer wife, yet he treats her as a thrall."

Mist was surprised that the older woman would voice aloud the very thoughts that were in her own mind. Knut's treatment of Iliana was nothing like how his own father treated his mother. She couldn't help but wonder what made the two so different. They were both warriors, but Finn had a code of ethics that his son was definitely lacking.

"Was theirs an arranged marriage?"

Edda hesitated, her look once again straying to the couple. "He chose her and she agreed," she answered carefully.

Mist understood what she was not saying. It was not a love match. She turned to where Valdyr was standing next to Finn and wondered if that was what was in store for her. Obviously Knut had desired Iliana in the beginning, but desire didn't last where love wasn't present, as well.

No. That would not be her life. For one thing, Valdyr was nothing like Knut. Watching him with Erika had convinced her of that. For another, she was not meek enough to allow herself to be so abused.

Instead of commenting on Edda's statement, Mist told her, "I am pleased that you and Iliana will be accompanying us to Egilsfjord. My sisters will love having you there, and especially little Cecilia."

Edda smiled sadly, tears turning her brown eyes into shimmering pools of reflected light. "Children are always a joy. I wish that I had been able to give my husband more children, but the gods decreed otherwise."

It was an opportunity to teach the older woman about the Lord Jesus, but Mist sensed it was not yet the time. She wrapped her arms around her bent knees and asked, "Your other son—how old is he?"

Bottom lip trembling slightly, Edda told her, "He *was* almost fifteen summers."

Realizing that she had brought up a painful subject, Mist touched Edda's arm in compassion. "There is still hope, Edda. Do not give up on him yet." She would pray for this lost son of Finn's. God willing, he was safe and would find his way back to his grieving family.

Sighing, Edda lifted her eyes to the lightening sky, blinking back tears. "Ours is a harsh life, Mist. We expect death, and learn to live with the thought of it." She slowly pushed herself to her feet, placing her hands against her lower back as she gradually straightened.

Edda joined her husband to say farewell, and Iliana came over to speak to Mist. The forced smile on the woman's face made Mist wonder just exactly what Knut had said to her, but she refrained from asking. If Iliana wanted to confide in her, she would, otherwise Mist would not pry.

Mist reached out for the babe, and Iliana placed her in Mist's waiting arms. Cuddling her close, Mist glanced at Iliana. The other woman was watching her husband with barely concealed hostility.

"Is everything well?" Mist asked.

Iliana straightened her shoulders as she turned Mist's way. She nodded. "Yes. Everything is well."

Valdyr approached them. "The fog has burned away. We are ready to sail. Finn's expedition party has already left and the others have started the trek to the farm."

Mist glanced up in surprise. So intent was she on playing with the babe, she hadn't even noticed their departure. Iliana hadn't even made a move when her husband left; sitting in stony silence.

Hastily getting to her feet, Mist told Valdyr, "We are ready."

Valdyr helped Iliana into the ship, and Mist handed her the babe before climbing in herself. Valdyr's large hands spanned her waist as he lifted her inside, settling her into the gently rocking ship. She caught his gaze, and something in his eyes made her stomach flip oddly. Frowning, she turned away and seated herself across from Iliana, but couldn't keep her attention from turning back to Valdyr as they pushed off from land.

Mist grew more excited as each stroke of the oar brought them closer to home. She had sorely missed her family and couldn't wait to see them again.

Valdyr felt the wind at his back, the smoothness of the ship as it skimmed along, and was oddly discontented. He had always been more at home on the sea than on the land, but something had changed, and he feared it had to do with the woman seated in the middle of his ship, her red hair reflecting sunlight as she searched the sea on either side of them for signs of sea life.

He joined her, but the ocean remained placid and empty, at least to the casual observer. In the depths, he knew there was a treasure trove of sustenance.

He glanced from Mist to Iliana and couldn't help but compare them. Mist's green eyes were full of fire and secrets that tempted a man to delve into them. Every time he looked into those glowing jewels, his whole being responded to the unintentional invitation he saw there. Iliana's eyes, while lovely, were subdued, and whatever fire there might have been had been reduced to mere ashes, likely from that scoundrel of a husband of hers.

Even hidden under layers of grimy ash, Iliana's clothes spoke of the wealth of her father-in-law, the once exquisite and colorful embroidery turned now to various shades of gray. Mist, on the other hand, did not flaunt her wealth. To the observant eye, one could see that the woolen and colorless kirtle she wore was of the finest quality, as were the brooches at her shoulders that held her apron in place. The colors she wore were earthy, much like the woman herself.

They made a good pair, he and Mist, as he chose for himself the same set of standards. If he couldn't receive respect as the man that he was, he didn't deserve it; he wasn't about to buy it with costly raiment and jewels.

His attention turned to Edda sitting next to her daughter-in-law, her thoughts obviously miles away with her husband. Now there was a man worthy of respect, and Valdyr didn't need Mist to tell him so. His concern for his people was exactly what a chieftain should provide. That the man had weathered some mighty fierce battles was proven by the scars he wore, and he wore them with pride.

The wind suddenly died and the men took up the oars once again. Their strokes were even and powerful, putting their muscle behind their rowing to get them to the farm before this night was finished. Gulls dipped and swayed overhead, their keen eyesight searching out the food that moved just below the water.

The sun was beginning to dip toward the horizon when Valdyr heard the horn that warned Egil of their approach.

They beached the boat on the shore near the farm and Egil was awaiting them. Valdyr wondered if Mist had even noticed that her father's once robust frame was much thinner than when Valdyr had first arrived and that there were dark circles under the elder man's eyes. Noticing Iliana and Edda, Egil's brows lifted slightly, but he said nothing.

Valdyr leaped from the ship into the water, then turned to help the women over the side. His eyes met Mist's and he saw the hesitation in them. She reluctantly placed her hands on his shoulders as he once again wrapped his hands around her waist. Her waist was so tiny, his fingers almost touched, and he felt again that desire to safeguard her from whatever perils she might face.

He forced himself to break their connection and lifted her out of the ship. She turned when he set her down and reached out to take the babe from Iliana, then approached her father.

"Welcome home, *dóttir.*"

Mist smiled. "Thank you, *Far.* I have brought company." She turned to introduce the women. "This is Lord Finn's wife, Edda, and her daughter-in-law, Iliana."

Egil's eyes narrowed. "Finn One Eye?"

At Egil's tone, Edda's voice wavered. "Yes, my lord. Our farm was destroyed by the volcano. He has gone to find another place farther inland where we can begin anew."

Egil glanced from Edda to Iliana, and then to the babe. He slowly nodded his head, his silence showing that his mind was busy figuring out the complexities of this unexpected turn of events. He finally gave a forced smile.

"Welcome, my ladies. My home is at your disposal."

Valdyr noticed Mist's shoulders relax, her relief evident. "And this, *Far*, is little Cecilia."

Unimpressed, Egil turned to a thrall standing at his side. "Show the women to the house." The look he gave Mist was undecipherable. "You go with them and introduce them to the family."

Mist glanced from her father to Valdyr suspiciously. Nodding, she told the women. "This way."

They followed behind her, and Egil watched until they were clearly out of hearing distance before turning to Valdyr.

"I was concerned about supplies before, but now moreso."

Valdyr frowned. "Is it as bad as that?"

"Worse."

Mist wondered what her father had to say to Valdyr, resenting the fact that he was treating Valdyr as though he was already head of the family.

She brushed aside her feelings and turned to Edda as they entered the small antechamber of the house. Mist had never seen Finn's farm and wondered how her father's compared. Would the women be comfortable here? They had little choice, but still, Mist wished for them to feel at home.

Brita glanced up from where she sat near the hearth, sewing a garment. She hastily rose to her feet, laying the garment aside.

"Mist! Welcome home!"

She quickly crossed the room, her eyes on Edda and Iliana.

"Brita, I would like you to welcome Edda and Iliana. They are from Reydarfjord on the other side of the island. Their farm was destroyed by the volcano and they will be staying here while Edda's husband searches out new land."

Brita ducked her head slightly in acknowledgment. "You are most welcome. Come inside near the fire. I will get you something to eat."

"Thank you, my lady," Edda answered. "We do not wish to cause you any trouble."

Brita's face softened. "Please, call me Brita, and it is no trouble at all."

Mist caught movement from the back of the house and saw Astrid coming toward them, Bjorn just behind her. Mist made the introductions once again.

Bjorn looked past her. "Valdyr?"

"He is at the ship talking to my father."

He left the house, and Mist turned to her sister. She had never seen Astrid looking lovelier. Her sister fairly glowed, the blue color of her tunic giving her eyes an extra sparkle. Mist cocked an eyebrow.

"Something has happened while we were away."

The statement invited an answer but Brita interrupted.

"Not now, Mist. Let us get our guests situated."

Brita was right, of course, but Mist couldn't help the shiver of disquiet that coursed through her. How was it that Valdyr seemed to be included in whatever was going on while she felt more like an outsider?

Astrid was walking next to Iliana, her eyes focused on the baby. "And who might this be?"

Iliana gave her a tired smile, pulling back the coverings from the babe's face. Large blue eyes in a cherubic face stared back at them.

"This is Cecilia."

Astrid began cooing to the baby, her matching blue eyes sparkling with delight. She gently pulled the covers back farther the better to see the child. "May I hold her?"

Iliana handed the child over without hesitation. "I am afraid that she is dirty right now," she said apologetically.

"I will change her, if you like." Astrid cuddled the babe close despite the reeking smell coming from the infant.

Iliana's face colored with embarrassment. Before she could speak, Mist told her sister, "They lost everything to the volcano."

Brita and Astrid stared at Iliana in sympathy, neither knowing what to say.

"I am certain that we can find something," Brita finally answered, and Astrid quickly agreed.

"Oh, yes. If you do not mind, I will take her and give her a bath and fresh clothing. We still have Erika's things from when she was a babe."

Just then, Erika popped in the door. At the sight of the newcomers, she stopped, her curious glance quickly scanning all of them before fixing on the babe in Astrid's arms. Eyes widening with delight, she hurried across the room.

"Ooh! A babe!"

Mist grinned at her niece's exuberance and made the introductions. When Astrid took Cecilia to change her, Erika was close on her heels.

"What a sweet child," Edda remarked softly.

Mist started to make a comment when she noticed

the sadness dimming Edda's brown eyes. She had to be thinking of her youngest son again. A sudden pall hung over the room. Just how many lives had been lost to that raging mountain?

Iliana and Edda wearily seated themselves on stools close to the hearth, and Brita brought them each a platter with bread and cheese. The thrall handed them each a wooden cup filled with buttermilk. Thanking them, they began to eat while Mist pulled her sister aside.

"Lord Finn will come for them after he has found a new home. I intend to try to get them to stay the winter."

Brita glanced back at the two. "It will make it crowded with all of Valdyr's men, and our supplies will be stretched."

"I know," Mist agreed, chewing nervously on her bottom lip. "I have begun praying that God will show me the answer."

"If He does," Brita said, picking up her discarded sewing, "then perhaps I will listen more to what you have to say about Him."

Surprised, Mist smiled in amusement. She doubted the Lord was willing to use bribery as a means of bringing His children to Him.

Mist turned when she heard the men coming in the door. Valdyr caught her eye, but made his way to where the weapons were stored, hanging his baldric on a wooden peg on the wall. The sword it contained was one of the largest and best made that she had ever seen. The runes etched into it gave it its ominous name: Cuts Deep.

At one time, she would have envied such a weapon, and truth to tell, she still felt pride in such an amazing piece. It only went to show just how much she had changed, but just how much more she had to do so before she would be a woman that the Lord would be proud to call His daughter. She wasn't certain she would ever reach that point that Drustan called *turning the other cheek*.

As the evening meal had already been served before they arrived, Brita and Gudrun placed bowls of *skyr*, the thick soured milk, on the table for those who had just returned, along with platters of cheese and bread. The famished men fell on the food with a ravenous hunger. Mist found herself unable to conjure up an appetite. She had too much on her mind, not least of which was her father's reaction to having guests for the winter. What had Valdyr told him anyway?

She located her father at the wooden table talking to several of the men. Taking her courage in hand, she approached him and waited until he acknowledged her. She might be the chieftain's daughter, but she knew her place.

When he glanced up, she asked, "May I speak with you, *Far*?"

She had lived with the man twenty-and-six summers and still couldn't read the expression on his impassive face. It had always been thus. How had her *mor* ever been able to penetrate that stoic shell of his?

He got to his feet and motioned for her to precede him outside.

Night had fallen and thousands of stars pierced through the undulating colors of the sky. The moon had risen and hung like a scythe in the darkening expanse.

Mist tried to think of a way to begin the conversation. In the end, her father did it for her.

"Valdyr tells me that Finn One-Eye saved your life. I thought you told me it was the Christian, Drustan." She didn't miss the suspicion in his voice.

"Both are true," she told him. "It was at the battle of Leuven that Finn saved my life." She hated talking about it. Her heart began to race, her breathing growing shallow as she told him the story. Even now, the mental picture had the power to turn her legs to jelled curd. "I was surrounded, three against one. I could only bury myself under my shield and await certain death." She remembered turning her face to the side from beneath the shield and seeing Finn roaring his way toward her, cleaving through his assailants like a knife cleaves through butter.

Her father's eyes were shining as she related the story and, for the first time, she could see the emotion in their depths. Surely those weren't tears.

"You never told me this," he told her huskily.

She folded her arms against her chest and looked up at the sky. It was easier to watch those mesmerizing patterns of dancing lights than to face her father's emotion.

"It is not something that I like to remember," she answered softly.

Egil sighed. "It is a debt of honor that I will gladly repay. You need to know, however, that our supplies will run out before spring."

She whirled to face him. "How can that be?"

"The ash from the volcano did more damage than we originally anticipated. We will more than likely have to slay several of the sheep and cattle before spring sets in."

Livestock was about the only thing that accounted for wealth on the island as there were no natural resources to depend on for trade. To diminish the livestock would diminish her father's ability to barter.

"I am sorry, *Far*."

He shrugged. "We will make do."

Mist turned to go back inside, her heart heavy. How much worse would it get when Finn's family arrived?

"Mist?"

She stopped and reluctantly turned back to face her father, her eyebrows raised in question.

"I am thankful that Finn saved your life." He paused, swallowing hard. "You are…you are very special to me."

Mist felt as though she had just been handed a new sword made of silver rather than iron. Her smile was warm.

"Thank you, *Far*."

"I want you to know that I have given my consent for Bjorn and Astrid to marry."

So that was why her sister was in such a jubilant mood. That was good news indeed.

"This makes no difference to the contract between you and Valdyr," he told her.

Such an idea had never occurred to her, so why was he mentioning it now? Did he think Valdyr would wish to be released? The thought didn't make her as happy as it should have.

"Although I will be proud to have Bjorn as a son, I still think Valdyr is the right man for you."

She might just agree with her father. But would Valdyr?

# Chapter 9

A little over two weeks later, Finn's weary family arrived at Egilsfjord.

Mist hastened outside to greet them, along with her father, Valdyr, Edda and Iliana. Mist was surprised that there was only one man in the group, and he was leading the entourage.

"Where are all the men, Olaf?" Edda asked him anxiously, looking past his shoulders. "Was there trouble?"

He swung the pack he was carrying over his shoulder and tiredly dropped it to the ground. "We passed a beached whale a few miles from here. The men stayed behind to slay and process it." He glanced at Valdyr. "If you would like to send some of your men, as well, I will show them the way."

Valdyr's men rose from their various places scattered around the farmyard where they had been enjoying the diminishing sunlight. Some were preparing their weapons for the coming winter's storage while others had been amusing themselves by challenging each other in games of strength. Excitement shone in their eyes. Anything out of the ordinary was a breath of fresh air.

Amund glanced at Valdyr. When Valdyr nodded his head in agreement, Amund began to rattle off orders to the men standing around.

Some quickly retreated into the house to get weapons that had already been stored, others searched out implements to help them in processing the meat.

"Take some horses and carts, as well," Egil told them, and several men hastened to obey. There would be too much meat for the men to carry, even with so many hands.

Valdyr turned to Egil. "I will go with them."

Sharing a look with Mist, he caught the ax that Amund threw to him without taking his eyes from hers. She thought she knew how a mouse must feel when confronted by a cat, every muscle frozen, unable to look away as it waited for the cat to pounce. The sudden gleam in Valdyr's eyes told her that he knew just what effect he was having on her, and her face set stonily as she stared back at him. The man was absolutely too sure of himself.

"Ready?" Amund asked.

Valdyr nodded, finally releasing her from his magnetic stare and, turning, he followed after Amund as he trotted after the others.

Mist let out a protracted breath, watching them until they disappeared over one of the hills that surrounded the farm, the memory of that look leaving her oddly shaken. For the first time in her life she understood how

Brita had felt when she watched her husband leave home on some expedition. Only Valdyr was not her husband, at least not yet. So why did she feel so bereft at his going? And why did thoughts of what his homecoming might bring make her heart beat faster? It was not like he and she would share the same kind of greeting as Brita did with her husband—a loving embrace, a passionate kiss—although she found the thought not as unpleasant as she would have several months ago.

Edda had already led her family into the house, their excited chatter bringing a smile to Mist's face as she pushed away thoughts of Valdyr and followed them inside. Weariness had vanished in the faces of Finn's people, to be replaced by delight at having finally reaching their destination and being reunited with the others. Shy younger children clung to their mother's skirts, while the older ones stared curiously about.

Brita had already prepared food and was setting it on the table. She glanced about and then questioned Mist in surprise.

"Where is everyone? I expected more people than this."

"Finn's men found a beached whale," Mist told her, helping her lay out the platters. "Some of our men have gone to help them process it."

Brita's blue eyes shone with excitement. "That will certainly relieve us of the worry of how we will feed everyone this winter."

The same thought had occurred to Mist. Even with their larger group, the meat from a good-size whale would feed them for a long time to come.

"I knew that God would take care of us," Mist told her sister, stepping back to survey the table.

Perhaps her voice lacked the conviction it should have for Brita's look was skeptical. Before Brita could reply, Edda joined them with several of the others.

Edda made the introductions of her clan. There was her niece, Finna, a young woman barely past her youth who was the daughter of Inga, Edda's sister-in-law, married to Finn's brother, Solvig. Dagrun was Inga's oldest daughter and Haldor her only son. There were others who hung back; Mist assumed they were thralls or servants. She had yet to be introduced to the men, and Mist wondered with some trepidation where they were going to house everyone.

Excited chatter quickly ceased as the group seated themselves and fell on the food. Brita set a pitcher of buttermilk on the table along with some wooden cups.

"Please, help yourselves. If you will excuse us, Mist and I were in the middle of making cheese. We need to get back to it before it spoils."

Edda started to climb to her feet, but Brita waved her away. "No, Edda. We can manage. You have some catching up to do with your family."

Reluctantly seating herself again, Edda gave them a doubtful frown. "If you are certain…"

"We are," Mist agreed, and Edda relented, thankful to find out news of those who had traveled overland instead of by ship as she had. Mist hadn't missed the worried frowns that often marked the older woman's face over the past few weeks as she stood in the doorway staring off into the distance, waiting for her family to be reunited once again. Such was the life of a wife. Mist had the feeling that when she married Valdyr, she would spend much of her time looking for his return, as well.

Brita and Mist returned to their cheesemaking while

the others had their meal. For the first time in a long
while they would have salted cheese, thanks to Valdyr.
He had brought several kegs of salt with him and, to
Mist at least, it was worth more than the emerald jew-
eled bracelet he had brought for her. A piece of jewelry
that, although was lovely, she still had yet to wear as it
so closely reminded her of a shackle.

"Mist?"

Busy stirring the rennet into the milk, Mist was paying little attention to her sister. "Hmm?"

"Do you really believe your God provided the whale?"

Mist paused, her mind already running ahead of itself
trying to figure out how to answer since she had never
had the opportunity to learn any of the scriptures. She
always felt so inept when questioned about her faith, but
decided that the best way was merely to tell Brita what
God's word said.

"God's holy book says that if you believe, you will
get what you ask for."

Brita's look held cynicism. "Every time?"

Mist thought about Jesus begging God to save him
from the cross. His answer had been no. She stopped
stirring and focused on her sister.

"If we ask within His will."

She could see by the look on her sister's face that she
was not satisfied with the answer. Mist sighed, not certain how to make things clear when she was so often
unclear herself. She noticed Erika talking to Finna and
decided to use her niece to clarify her thoughts.

"Let me try to explain it another way," she started,
and Brita took over stirring the cheese. Relieved, Mist
wiped her hands on a towel to clear them of the oily
residue.

"If Erika asked you for something that you felt would cause her injury, you would refuse her, would you not?"

Brita's look turned pensive. "You mean like the time she asked me for a knife when she was but three years old?"

It was hard not to grin at the reminder of her niece's indomitable spirit. "Just so!" Mist agreed emphatically. "You told her no."

Brow creased in thought, Brita slowly nodded. "I understand, but what about asking for fair weather, or food for the winter? How can this not be in His will?"

Mist bit her lip. "I do not know the mind of God, Brita. Sometimes His answer is yes, sometimes no and sometimes, wait."

Brita pursed her lips thoughtfully, but before they could continue their conversation, Edda interrupted them.

"We would like to help."

Brita and Mist turned to her in surprise and noticed that the food had been cleared from the table. Iliana and Inga were standing behind her, holding the dishes.

"That is not necessary," Brita began, but Edda held up a hand.

"If we are to share in the bounty, then we need to help. Besides—" she smiled "—many hands make less work."

Mist frowned. "But surely the others are tired after their long journey."

Inga shook her head. "We were able to rest on the way. We would like to help. What can we do?"

Mist and Brita exchanged glances, and Brita shrugged. Mist knew that she would feel the same in their place.

"This batch is almost ready to fit into the molds," Brita said, handing them the wooden forms used for setting the cheese.

Without further explanation, the women began to gather the necessary supplies, moving as one. Mist grinned, shaking her head. It was obvious that they had their own way of doing things and that they were used to working together.

Inga called her daughter over. "Finna, we need more wood for the fire." She glanced at Brita. "Where can she find some?"

Brita turned to Mist. "I almost forgot. I was going to ask you if you would gather some. We are running low, and we will need more to finish the cheese."

"I will take the cart and go inland," Mist answered.

"Finna will go with you," Inga told her.

When Mist pulled her sword and baldric from its peg on the wall, Finna's brows lifted in astonishment. Mist realized that it would take a more modest person than herself to be unmoved by the look of admiration and awe the girl gave her. Swallowing down her swelling pride, she ducked out the door into the bright sunlight.

She searched the farmyard, wondering where her father had disappeared to. He hadn't gone with the others, nor had he come inside. She decided he was probably close by, checking on the animals.

Finna followed her to where they kept the small hand-pulled cart for transporting goods. Mist stowed her sword in the cart and lifted the tongue by the handle, surprised that her strength had returned enough to allow her to move it with ease. It was good to finally feel more like her old self.

As they walked along, Finna peppered her with questions, especially once she found out that Mist had been with Finn in two of his battles.

The wooden wheels of the cart bumped and rattled

over the rocky ground as they pulled it along. It took them some time to reach the tree line, and Mist realized that they would have to hurry if they were going to make it back in time to bring Brita the needed wood. Still, she took the time to savor the peace of one of her favorite spots. The screech of a white hawk pierced the still morning air as it flew high in the sky overhead, searching for prey. Small birch trees still dotted the landscape, and the melted ice from an inland glacier rushed over the hill, spilling out into a thundering waterfall and then onward to the sea by a twisting, winding river.

But Finna was staring awestruck at the majestic sight of the impressive waterfall. Mist couldn't blame her; it stuck her the same way every time she came here. Despite its many drawbacks, she never got tired of the island's rugged beauty.

After they had been working for some time, they seated themselves on the hard ground, their backs against the rock face of the hill. Mist pulled out a small bag of bread and cheese.

Finna's chatter as they ate allowed Mist's mind to wander to thoughts of Valdyr. The connection between them was something she didn't understand, but she felt it growing stronger every day. It was becoming harder to imagine her life without him. When he was gone, the energy in the room went with him. In such a short time, he had embedded himself into the very fabric of her being.

When they had finished their meal, Mist got up and dropped the bag into the back of the cart, brushing her hands against her kirtle to free them of clinging crumbs.

"We had better hurry and finish," Mist warned, noticing the descending sun. Finna agreed, and they both set about clearing the area of as much brush as they could find.

"Be careful," Mist warned as Finna clambered up the steep hillside in search of larger pieces of wood.

She bent to check a crack she had noticed earlier in the wooden wheel, hoping that the wheel would last until they reached home. Finna's scream brought Mist upright, her heart pounding with dread. She whirled to see Finna slithering down the rocky hillside, scattering loose rocks as she came, a look of pure terror on her face.

At the top of the hill, roaring in challenge, was the largest white bear Mist had ever seen. Her first thought was that Valdyr had been wrong; the creature had not left the island or been slain by one of the other settlements. The next thought was that she was foolish not to have brought a long spear with her.

The blood seemed to congeal in her veins, freezing her into immobility as the animal dropped to all fours and began lumbering after Finna.

Another scream from Finna startled Mist into action. Grabbing the sword from the cart, she lunged forward, issuing the battle cry she had used when charging onto the battlefield. Hot blood charged through her veins as her mind came into sharp focus. Without further thought, she ran directly into the path of the charging bear.

She sent a prayer heavenward, certain that she was about to meet her God face-to-face, for there was no way that her light sword would penetrate the dense hide of the bear enough to slay him.

Valdyr watched the men load the last of the whale meat onto the carts. They might get tired of the brined meat before the winter was over, but at least they wouldn't starve.

He inhaled as a cool breeze blew across his sweat-soaked garments. Several of the men were gathering whale bone to be used for carving in the coming winter months when darkness would force them inside for most of the day. Nothing would be wasted of this bounty sent to them from the sea.

Amund joined him as the wagons began the return trip. They followed along behind, weary, yet pleased with their good fortune.

"We need to prepare the ship for winter," Amund suggested.

Valdyr nodded. "Egil has a boathouse we can use, although he tore apart his ship and used the wood for other things."

Valdyr thought it rather foolish to destroy your one means of transportation off this island but, then again, wood was scarce here. He decided that if he stayed, whatever the need, he would not destroy his ship.

"I will set some of the men to work on it as soon as we return," Amund told him.

Valdyr glanced at the sun and knew that it would begin its descent soon. The daylight hours were growing shorter each day, and the long darkness would soon be upon them. He was concerned about how his men were going to face the long hours with so few entertainments and no women to keep them company. Past experience didn't bode well for the future's peace.

Amund's quiet voice penetrated his reflections.

"I thought we had seen the last of him."

Valdyr followed his look and saw what had caught the other man's attention. The tracks of a large bear were imprinted into the wet ground, too near the farm for Valdyr's liking.

"They are fresh," Amund said, bending down and measuring the size of the print against his own large hand. If the prints were any indication, the creature was massive.

"He will need to be hunted," Valdyr said.

Amund agreed. They would have to retrieve weapons more suitable to such a quest, though, for going against such a beast with nothing but a sword would be foolhardy.

They reached the farm and, as had been his wont lately, the first thing he did was search out Mist. When he couldn't find her, he felt a vague disquiet that he tried to brush aside.

"Mist is not here?" he asked Brita.

Something in his voice must have alerted her. She set aside the round of cheese she had been salting, her face pensive. "Is something amiss?"

He debated whether to tell her or not and then realized that everyone needed to be made aware of the danger.

"We spotted the tracks of a large bear near the farm."

Her eyes widened, the color draining from her face. He felt his heart plunge with a premonition of what she was about to say.

"Mist and Finna went to gather wood."

Valdyr tried to rein in his panic. More than likely the bear had taken a separate path from the two women. Still, he couldn't completely stifle the fear that was trying to swell through him.

"How long ago?"

"Several hours." Brita's voice was a mere whisper.

"Did she take a weapon?"

"Only her sword."

Valdyr blew out a breath. That paltry weapon would be no deterrent against such a creature.

Amund joined them, handing Valdyr his bow, arrows and spear. One blond brow cocked upward. "Is something amiss?"

"Mist and the girl, Finna, have gone inland," Valdyr told him heavily.

Amund's face settled into grim lines. He hoisted his bag of arrows over his shoulder. "Then we had better hurry."

They didn't waste any time. As soon as they were free of the rocked compound they set out at a run. If Mist had been gone several hours, she was way ahead of them.

It soon became apparent from the tracks that the bear was following Mist and Finna. Valdyr had never held with the idea of deities, but he now took a moment to ask for Mist's safety from every one he could remember, including the one she believed in. Valdyr didn't know His name, but he petitioned Him nevertheless.

The sun was already near the horizon when they topped a hill and came upon a scene that turned his blood to ice.

With nothing but her sword, Mist stood facing one of the largest bears he had ever seen. The whooshing arc of the blade forced the enraged beast to retreat, but only temporarily. There was blood on the bear and on Mist, and Valdyr wasn't certain who it belonged to. The bear would charge forward, and Mist would thrust her sword at the only vulnerable spot that was available. It was then that Valdyr realized that the blood was coming from the bear's nose, which only enraged the animal further. Before long, the bear's fury would overcome its pain and then nothing would stop it.

"By my beard!" Amund whispered in horror.

One massive paw swiped the sword from Mist's hand, sending it skittering across the rocky ground, and Valdyr suddenly catapulted into action. With a bone-chilling war cry, he charged down the hill, pulling an arrow from the quiver and nocking it onto the bow as he ran.

Everything seemed to move in slow motion after that. Both the bear and Mist turned to face Valdyr. With that split second of opportunity, Valdyr sent the arrow unerringly toward its target. The arrow pierced through the bear's eye. It reared up, pawing at the arrow. A second arrow followed swiftly from behind Valdyr, embedding itself into the bear's heart. With a roar, the animal staggered backward before finally collapsing to the ground in a thundering heap.

Valdyr didn't stop running until he reached Mist's side. Knowing that Amund would finish what they had started, Valdyr didn't bother to see if the creature was truly dead. Instead, he threw down his bow and grabbed Mist, pulling her into his arms. She clung to him as tightly as moss clung to rock, and he couldn't tell if the trembling he felt was hers or his.

He had to bend to hear her quavering words. "You found us."

Tucking her head under his chin, he tightened his hold. "Of a certainty," he agreed, his voice growing huskier as he thought of what might have been. "There is nowhere that you can go where I will not find you."

He felt her tense at the intimidating words that he had meant only to be reassuring, and he reluctantly allowed her to ease back from his tight hold. She must have been truly in shock for she had no words.

Valdyr lifted her arm where blood covered her sleeve, and he felt his own blood drain from his face. She followed his look.

"It is not mine," she told him, her voice quivering with reaction.

"You are not injured?" he asked, still searching, and she shook her head.

When he finally looked down into her tear-laden eyes, he forgot Amund's presence, he forgot the bear, he forgot everything but the feel of her in his arms.

When he lowered his head, she didn't pull away as he expected. Instead, she leaned into his kiss, her lips tentative and exploring. When she clutched his tunic as though it was some kind of lifeline, he had to leash the powerful feelings that surged through him, afraid that he would frighten her with their intensity. He sensed that although she would courageously face a bear with nothing but a broadsword, that courage would fail her when faced by the feelings that seemed to be growing between them every day.

"That was the bravest thing I have ever seen!"

Finna's excited voice broke them apart as she came out of her hiding place behind the cart, and Mist quickly pulled out of his embrace. She once again retreated behind a cool reserve that firmly put Valdyr at a safe distance. Valdyr caught Amund's amused expression and gave him a look that warned him it would be wise to keep silent.

"So," Amund asked, "who gets this impressive pelt?"

## Chapter 10

The onset of winter came with a roaring storm system. One day the weather was fair and warm, the next icy winds blasted through the island, bringing with them a bone-wrenching cold. The fiery mountain had finally settled into silence, and its top once again became covered in snow.

Edda continued to fret over Finn's absence, and the longer he delayed, the more concerned Mist became, as well.

Iliana, on the other hand, seemed perfectly content without her husband. It wasn't the first time Mist had seen a loveless marriage, but it certainly wasn't something she would wish on her friend. Although divorce was practiced often by her people, contracts made between families often kept partners together when they might have otherwise split. She had long ago decided that there would never be a divorce for her since Drustan had told her that it was something God hated. It also made her more leery of entering into such a relationship if she couldn't be assured of the outcome. Just because she didn't believe in divorce didn't mean that Valdyr would agree.

The daylight hours had shortened until there were only a few each day now. Although everyone thought of ways to keep themselves occupied, boredom was never far away, especially for men used to physical activity. The besting contests were the main way the men exerted some of their stored energy. Tempers grew short and, if not for Valdyr's commanding presence, Mist had no doubt fights would have ensued when arguments erupted over who was the winner of such games.

Mist sat huddled under the white bear pelt that Valdyr had tanned and then presented to her. Since she hadn't slain the bear in the first place, she didn't think she deserved such a fine gift; however, Valdyr had disagreed with her. The honest admiration in his eyes had given her ego a much-needed boost.

She glanced around the room, yearning for the long days of summer when she could go to her thinking spot. Alone. With everyone having to stay close to the farm, she was constantly surrounded by people.

Her father was at the big table sharing horns of mead with the men, all except Bjorn, who was sitting with Astrid, presumably discussing their wedding that would occur in the spring, and Valdyr, who was sitting near the fire sharpening the heads of his arrows.

Mist was thrilled for her sister, knowing that Astrid had found true love. Her father had finally bowed to the inevitable and agreed to their marriage. Since their union would join the two families, there was no longer any need for Mist to join herself to Valdyr. The thought didn't please her as she had expected it to, and it didn't take much reasoning to understand why; she was very near to falling in love with Valdyr. She had known it the moment his arms had wrapped around her after slaying the bear. The overwhelming feeling of having come home left her shaken.

A rapping at the door startled her and brought instant silence to the room. The darkness made it dangerous to be out and about, especially on a moonless night. The thought that one of the servants might be injured had Mist pushing away the pelt and scrambling to her feet to answer it. Out of the corner of her eye she saw Valdyr rise to his feet, as well.

She threw back the door, catching her breath as a gust of icy wind rushed in. Someone was lurking in the shadows, but Mist couldn't make out the features until he stepped into the light. She opened the door wider and stepped back.

"Lord Finn," she said in surprise.

The man looked weary and half-frozen. Motioning him inside, Mist quickly shut the door behind him.

A squeal had Finn looking past her shoulder, a tired smile curling his mouth as Edda hastened across the room. Mist hurriedly stepped aside to allow the excited woman to pass, smiling as she threw herself into her husband's arms.

The room once again broke into excited chatter as Egil came forward to greet their guest. When Egil held out his arm, Finn grasped it at the forearm while keeping his other arm firmly around his wife's substantial waist.

"Welcome, my friend," Egil told him.

"Come closer to the fire, Lord Finn," Mist encouraged, and Finn followed her into the room.

Iliana looked past his shoulder before she turned questioning eyes his way.

"Knut has decided to stay with Balder at Straumfjord."

Finn and Valdyr shared a knowing look, and Valdyr gave a slight nod of acknowledgment. Valdyr glanced Mist's way, and she once again felt the warmth of his protection, just like those moments when he had held her in his arms and assured her that there was nowhere she could go that he would not find her. Was Valdyr's concern emotionally motivated or merely a form of possession? She didn't think that he would readily give up something that he thought belonged to him.

Had the kiss they shared meant as much to him as it had to her? It was that kiss more than anything that had helped her to realize it would be no hardship to be wed to such a man. If only he was a child of the Christ, she knew she would have willingly given her heart to him long ago.

Mist saw that instead of being distressed at her husband's absence, Iliana looked relieved. She couldn't blame the woman. Mist would rather face an army on a battlefield than be married to such a one.

Finn's family gathered around him, anxiously waiting to hear what he had to say.

"I found us a place. We have built a small house, and I left the men behind to watch over it while I came to get you." His face set into immovable lines. "It is not the best land, but it was the best that I could do."

"But, Lord Finn," Mist objected. "How will you survive with no supplies to last you the winter?"

"A good question," Egil inserted, turning his look once more on Finn. Mist could see that her father had something on his mind, possibly a solution to Finn's problem.

Finn's mouth set firmly. "We will manage." He held his hands out to the fire, refusing to look at his wife.

Edda looked dismayed, but remained silent. She would do whatever her husband decreed, not merely to obey, but because of the deep love and commitment she so often showed toward him. That was the kind of marriage Mist had always hoped to have. She only hoped that Finn's pride wouldn't cause his family to suffer.

"I have a suggestion," Egil told him. Finn paused while Egil seated himself on the stool beside him. He waited to hear what Egil had to say, but his look was hardly encouraging.

"I have a tenant farm near here..."

"I will not be some man's chattel," Finn told him harshly, rising to his feet. The flickering flames of the fire highlighted his forbidding features, his good eye gleaming with his anger. The scar on his face stood out in sharp relief as a tide of hot color rushed into his face.

Egil slowly rose to face him, his irritation at having been interrupted clearly evident. Egil scowled at him. "You did not let me finish."

The two men glared at each other like two dogs, their hackles raised, fighting over the same bone. Somehow, there had to be a way for the two to compromise to everyone's satisfaction.

"Let us hear what Lord Egil has to say," Edda pleaded softly. Finn looked down at her, and the hardness left his face. He turned back to Egil.

"My pardon. Please, say what is on your mind."

They grudgingly resumed their seats, and Mist fought back a grin. No wonder she had always admired Finn; he reminded her much of her father.

"As I was saying," Egil began, "I have a tenant farm several miles distant that has been left fallow since the previous tenant decided to go back to Norway."

Finn folded his arms but remained silent.

"My daughter has told me that she owes her life to you." When Finn opened his mouth, Egil held up a hand. "I do not have enough gold, silver, furs or anything else to repay you for such a service. No amount of tribute in the world would do so," Egil choked, and Finn's hard features softened as he realized that Egil was speaking from his heart.

"I would like to *give* that land to you."

Edda sucked in a breath, her hand tightening on Finn's shoulder. Finn glanced up at Edda, reaching up to place his larger hand over hers, but quickly returned his attention to Egil.

"That is a generous offer, but one I cannot accept. I may have saved Mist's life once or twice, but she returned the favor tenfold with my men."

Egil's mouth set uncompromisingly. "Be that as it may, it is a debt I fully intend to repay. And there is another benefit in it for me. Having a man such as yourself so near assures me of even greater safety. I believe we could come to some kind of understanding."

Mist sighed in relief. A *vinfengi*! Of course. A contract based upon friendship, much as that that existed between Egil and Valdyr's father. A *vinfengi* was even more binding than the marriage contract brokered between her father and Valdyr's.

She could see Finn considering what her father was

suggesting. As land became more scarce, those seeking to hang on to what they had would need all the help they could get. Together, they would control a large portion of the southern part of the island where the grazing was at its best.

"Of course," Egil continued, "the farm has been sitting idle for many months and will need some work to make it habitable again." He suddenly took an interest in his fingernails. "You are welcome to stay here until springtime," he suggested.

Mist could see that Finn was about to object until he looked around at his family, their hopeful expressions bringing a quick frown to his face.

"Give me a night to think on it," Finn suggested with less enthusiasm than Mist had hoped for.

Egil relaxed against his seat. "Of course. Let me know your decision in the morning."

Mist noticed Valdyr's set face. No doubt he would have something to say in regards to Knut.

When everyone had sought their pallets for the night, Mist lay in her spot listening to the whispering voices around her. She couldn't make out the words, but she had no doubt of what was being discussed. After several hours of wakefulness, she finally got to her feet when she heard Brita stirring about. As they began to prepare the food for the day, Iliana joined them. Mist smiled, and handed her the quern for grinding the wheat.

"Could you not sleep, either?"

She shook her head, the dark circles under eyes telling their own story.

They worked in companionable silence until everyone was awake and moving about. When the sun eventually rose, everyone hastened to use the opportunity of the few hours of daylight to get their chores done. There was little to do outside except feed and water the wintered stock that were safely ensconced in their barns.

Inside, there was much more to be done. The women were busy spinning and carding the sheep's wool, repairing and sewing garments.

Brita was adding embroidery to the hem of a new dress for Astrid while Mist pressed wrinkles out of the freshly washed clothing on the clothing board. Mist envied Brita her patience and expertise, and she loved the final result, but she herself had never had the persistence to learn the complicated stitches.

"Valdyr is a fine man," Brita said without looking up from her work.

Where had that come from? Brows furrowed, Mist told her, "So you said before."

Brita finally met her eyes, and Mist was taken aback by the determination in them.

"It is obvious to everyone that you have feelings for the man. Why are you trying so hard to hide it?"

Mist felt chilled clear through. Was this true? She glanced surreptitiously around but didn't see anyone looking their way. Catching her sister's eye once again, she shrugged.

"He is not a Christian."

Brita's needlework fell to her lap, her mouth dropping open in astonishment. Brita's voice rose several octaves. "That is why you are keeping him at arm's length?"

Irritated at her sister's inability to understand the devotion she felt to her Lord, she snapped back, "Yes. That is why."

Mist couldn't miss the sadness that crept into her sister's eyes as she slowly shook her head. "Life is short,

Mist. No one knows that better than me. Don't let your stubbornness deny you a chance at happiness."

She needed no one to tell her how short life was. It was the very thing that helped her to focus, not on this life, but the one to come.

"That is what I have been trying to tell you since I came back from Norway," she reminded Brita softly.

Both busy with their own thoughts, they dropped into silence.

Mist glanced up from the pressing board and saw Finn and Edda approaching her father later in the day. Mist exchanged a look with Brita, and they both continued their work while stretching their ears to overhear the conversation.

Egil motioned for them to have a seat, and pushed a plate of bread and cheese toward them.

Finn cleared his throat as though the words he wanted to say were lodged inside.

"I have decided to accept your offer, on one condition."

Egil tensed, and Mist closed her eyes, a sigh escaping in frustration. This was not an auspicious way to begin a conversation with her father. He slowly looked up, his face set in a determined line.

"I wish to pay for the land and purchase a few of your livestock to begin my own herds again."

Egil leaned back, glancing curiously from one to the other. "And how did you intend to pay? It was my understanding that you lost everything."

"Not quite everything," Finn stated and turned to Edda.

Edda reached behind her neck and unfastened a necklace that had been hidden beneath her tunic. She pulled it forth and the movement of the silver coins caught the light from the fire, sending glittering prisms dancing about the room.

Mist's wide eyes matched those of her father.

As Edda handed him the necklace, Egil slowly reached out and allowed the silver to glide through his fingers. He looked at Finn in question.

"They are Arabic dirhems. It is how the Muslim people trade. Instead of trading with goods, they use coins to purchase items."

A gleam entered Egil's eyes, although Mist didn't understand the concept behind such an exchange. What good were silver coins here on this island? You couldn't eat them; you couldn't wear them. They were nothing more than an ostentatious show of wealth.

"How did you come by them?" Egil asked, not yet returning them.

"They were given to me as tribute."

Which meant that Finn had received them on one of his many raids down the European coast. Mist felt a keen disappointment in the man.

Egil glanced up, slowly closing his hand around the necklace as he studied both Finn and Edda. He finally nodded to Finn. "I will accept them in exchange for some of my livestock, but the farm is still yours as a gift."

The two men stared at each other, and Mist held her breath. Finally, Finn reached out his hand, sealing the deal by clasping Egil's forearm.

## Chapter 11

Each day the men went to the fjord where the stockfish were plentiful. When they returned, they would spend hours processing and wind drying them. The stockfish had become a staple here and abroad, and they were worth a lot as trading goods. The dried fish would keep almost indefinitely, making them easy to transport long distances across the seas.

Since the beached whale had increased their stored supplies for the winter, Egil was able to give Finn several head of sheep and cattle in exchange for the coin necklace without worrying about running short of supplies himself. It bothered Mist that her father had taken Finn's one source of supplying his family after losing everything else, but Finn was right; you couldn't eat silver coins.

What exactly her father was going to do with the coins she had no idea. Perhaps when the traders came in the spring they would be willing to accept them in exchange for the goods they would need. If not, she could see no purpose in keeping them except for their shining beauty. And again, you could not eat beauty.

Valdyr began to seek Mist out more often when she wasn't busy, encouraging her to play a game of chess or *hnefatfl* with him. She enjoyed their verbal sparring at such times; she especially loved seeing the little crinkled laugh lines that fanned out around his eyes when he grew amused at her attempts to defeat him. She knew that he was trying to woo her, and her heart thrilled at his gentle attempts, but her mind warned her about allowing things to get out of hand.

Each day her feelings for him grew, yet she still held herself aloof. The disparity between his paganism and her growing faith cooled the feelings warming her heart. She used these opportunities to speak about Jesus with him and, while he didn't forbid her to, neither did he encourage her.

His intelligent questions were beginning to frustrate her as she was unprepared to give him the answers he was seeking. If only there was some way that he could talk to Drustan, she just knew that he could be made to see the truth as she had. Only then would she allow her feelings to escape from their cage.

Two weeks came and went since Finn's appearance when one day unwelcome visitors appeared at the farm.

Valdyr was sitting on a rock outside enjoying the few hours of daylight despite the cold temperatures, which were much warmer than his home in Norway. The sky was wanly lit by the sun, bands of gray and blue almost disappearing into the horizon line of the darker blue sea.

Knut arrived unexpectedly, the companion at his side one Valdyr had never seen before but assumed must be the one called Balder. Valdyr tensed, instant antipathy toward Knut bringing a low rumble from his throat. They hadn't yet spotted him, and his eyes narrowed at their clandestine actions, making him wonder just exactly what they could be up to.

Valdyr rose to his feet, glancing quickly at the swords hanging at the young men's waists beneath their fur mantles. His own sword was hanging inside the house on its peg, so he would have to face them unarmed except for his sax, the small knife he always carried with him. Knowing the weak caliber of men they were, the thought disturbed him less than it might have otherwise.

"What is it you wish here?" he called out to them sharply, and they jerked to a stop, their eyes widening in surprise at his unexpected presence.

The two briefly shared a look before Knut quickly regained his poise, placing one hand on the sword at his side. "I have come to visit with my wife and daughter."

Knut's earlier lack of concern for his wife and daughter made Vadyr doubt his statement. He folded his arms across his chest in a decidedly unfriendly manner. Regardless of his doubts, the men had traveled a long way through darkness and cold to get here. The demands of hospitality would decree that they be made welcome, in spite of his reservations.

Before Valdyr could decide his next move, Finn exited the farm house with Edda, Iliana and Mist. Valdyr didn't miss the look of unease that crossed Iliana's face when she saw her husband, and neither had Mist. She placed a comforting hand on Iliana's shoulder and exchanged a concerned look with Valdyr. Whether the concern was for her friend or herself he wasn't certain, but as long as he was around, she didn't need to worry on either account. Surprised that no one else came out to join them, Valdyr wondered if Finn had ordered the other family members to remain inside.

"I have come to see Iliana," Knut told his father, and Valdyr saw the older man tense at Knut's belligerence.

Finn gave him a skeptical look. "I thought I told you to stay away from here until I sent for you."

"But you didn't send for me," Knut told him in a voice laced with bitterness.

Valdyr knew that with his next words the other man was about to unleash a tide of recriminations and hard feelings. Finn's acceptance of Egil's offer of land would be seen as choosing others over his own son, despite the fact that Knut had already informed his father that he was leaving the island.

"Our plans have changed," Finn told him.

"So I heard, but *my* plans have not."

A vague disquiet unsettled Valdyr. How had the other man heard about his father's plans?

Egil, Brita, Bjorn and Astrid came from the house and stood near the doorway. Balder straightened, fixing his look on Astrid and ignoring everyone else.

"Greetings, Astrid," he called.

Even from a distance Valdyr couldn't miss the lust gleaming in the man's eyes. Men had gone to war over less, and Bjorn's posture indicated that he was inclined in that direction.

Astrid leaned closer to Bjorn, and he wrapped his arm firmly around her waist. Valdyr noticed that his brother had armed himself before coming outside. He doubted that Knut and Balder were foolish enough to try anything when so sorely outnumbered, but his brother was obviously taking no chances.

"What are *you* doing here, Balder?" Egil asked coolly.

Balder motioned toward Knut. "I have come with my oath brother, who wishes to see his wife and child," he replied. "We have come a long way to do so."

Knut turned in his mother's direction, his eyes glittering with anger. "Are you not pleased to see me, *Mor*?"

Edda's face filled with uncertainty as she glanced from Finn to Knut. Clearly torn between her love of the two, she twisted her hands in her apron.

"Of course, my son," she answered him.

Knut raised an eyebrow at Iliana. "And you, my wife?"

Iliana's face drained of all color. Knut stretched out his hand, motioning for her to come to him. She hesitated, but then made her way to her husband. He wrapped her in a tight hug and whispered something in her ear. Valdyr could see real fear enter her eyes.

"There is not much daylight left," Knut reminded them all. "I would like to take a walk with my wife, and perhaps, if you are willing, spend the night here."

His attitude let them know that he was doing so whether they were willing or not. If not for the fact that Finn and Egil had forged a *vinfengi*, Valdyr knew Egil would have sent them on their way.

"You may stay in the barn." Egil's glaring look fixed on Balder. "Both of you."

"Your hospitality is lacking somewhat, Lord Egil," Balder chided.

"Mayhap because I do not feel very hospitable," Egil returned.

Balder glanced at Astrid, who refused to give him even a fleeting look. "As you wish." He shrugged.

Brita placed her hand on Egil's arm. "Perhaps they are hungry, *Far*," she remonstrated softly, reminding him of the rules of hospitality.

Balder gave her a wry smile. "Brita *in kyra*," he said quietly, and Brita turned to him sharply, color flaming into her cheeks.

Brita the gentle. From the tone of his voice, Balder meant it as a genuine compliment, and Valdyr wondered how he could possibly know about her if he had never met her before. He again felt that unease. Someone from the farm was feeding them information.

"Then give them something to eat," Egil snarled, and retreated into the house.

Bjorn pulled Astrid in after him, and the rest of Finn's family rushed out of the house to greet Knut.

"I will get you something to eat," Brita told the men. When they started to follow her inside, Finn barked at them to remain where they were.

Throwing Finn looks of remonstrance, everyone found seats either on benches, rocks or the cold, hard ground. They shivered from the biting cold, but refused to leave until they had a chance to greet Knut.

Valdyr noticed Mist slip away from the farm and decided to follow her.


Mist stared at the reflected image of the waning sun in the dark waters of the fjord. She was aware when Valdyr came to sit on the bank beside where she stood.

"Why are some men the way they are?" she asked aloud, not really expecting an answer.

She glanced at Valdyr and found him silently watching her. A cold breeze stung her cheeks and tousled his hair, but he seemed impervious to the freezing temperatures. He pulled up one leg and rested an arm on his upraised knee. He shrugged. "You are referring to Knut?"

Nodding, she moved to sit beside him. The biting cold from the ground penetrated her wool dress and made her shiver. She pulled her mantle closer around her shoulders, burying her chin beneath the collar.

"His mother and father are good people," Mist told him, though he had probably figured that out for himself.

"It would seem his choice of friends is not."

Thinking of Balder, she couldn't help but agree.

"God's holy word says that bad company spoils good morals."

Valdyr straightened, a frown drawing down his brows. "Their holy book truly says that?"

She gave a nod, a frosty haze forming where her breath met the cold air. The problem was, where her people were concerned, morality was a matter of interpretation.

Valdyr pulled a strange face. "It would be a happy circumstance if we could be certain that what they say is true. I once heard a priest talk about this heaven where their God lives." He turned to stare at the sinking sun. "It sounded like a…a peaceful place."

Mist straightened, all at once forgetting the cold. Had that been longing she heard in his voice? She surreptitiously studied him from beneath lowered lashes. His face in profile looked less intimidating than when confronting him head-on. She had the strongest urge to reach across and touch his jawline, his blond beard tinted with a red reflection of the sunset.

"I saw the words myself," she told him quietly.

He glanced at her sharply. "You can read their language?"

Discomfited at her unintentional blunder, Mist shook her head. "No...but Drustan read them to me."

She wondered at the sudden darkening of his eyes.

"You spent a lot of time with this Drustan. Perhaps he had ulterior motives in convincing you."

She realized what he was suggesting. "He is a man of God," she told him.

"But still a man," Valdyr warned in a soft voice.

Mist recognized the jealousy threading through his words. The thought that Drustan could be like other men almost made her chuckle. His bald pate and wrinkled features came clearly to mind. She gave Valdyr an amused smile. "He is older than my father."

The return smile on his face took her aback, for it hinted at hidden secrets and meanings that she, as a woman, could not possibly understand.

"Age has nothing to do with it," he told her drily.

She blinked at him, the confident smile sliding from her face, her mind uneasily accepting and discarding various thoughts that chased through it. The one that finally settled brought a return to equanimity. Drustan was a man of God, who had freely taken vows of celibacy to serve the God he loved so much. Unless Valdyr could meet the man, he wouldn't be able to understand that. She decided to change the uncomfortable subject.

"I do not believe that Knut came here to see Iliana."

Valdyr didn't answer for a moment. His face set sternly. He pushed one fist into his palm, the cracking of his knuckles loud in the stillness around them. "Those were my thoughts, as well."

"I believe that Balder convinced him to come so that Balder could see Astrid."

Valdyr turned toward her, and she saw his shoulders relax slightly. "I had not considered that."

"Why did you think he had come?" she asked.

He didn't immediately answer her question. When he did, the heated words took her by surprise.

"To bring you harm."

Strange that that thought had never even entered her mind. Knut might hate her, but she couldn't imagine him ever following through with that hate. He was singularly lacking in courage. She shook her head. "You see threats where none exist."

He took her by the chin and turned her to face him. Their eyes met and held for a long moment. "And you do not see what is right in front of your eyes."

She had the distinct feeling that he was no longer talking about Knut. When his gaze focused on her lips, she could feel them begin to tingle. He moved closer, dropping his arm until both hands rested on either side of her hips.

As Valdyr closed the distance between them, Mist found she was imprisoned by her own mounting feelings. Despite her admonishments to herself to keep a distance, her defenses crumbled beneath the look of his glowing blue eyes.

When his lips touched hers, she forgot all her reasons for denying him. Despite her resistance, she was falling in love with him and longed with all of her being for him to love her, as well.

It was Valdyr who suddenly brought a halt to their escalating encounter. He pulled back, stroking a thumb over her trembling lips. "Know this, Mist," he told her huskily. "I will let nothing happen to you *or* your family."

What was he thinking that turned his eyes to ice and brought such a deadly look to his face? She shivered, and he tugged her mantle closer against her chin. "You are cold," he said. The look on his face changed to one of amusement. "Mayhap you would like to share the *sowna* with me?" he teased.

Hot color rushed into her face at his suggestion, and she jumped to her feet, brushing the icy snow from her mantle to keep from looking Valdyr in the eyes. "I think not," she told him firmly, and felt her face warm even further at his rich chuckle. He was amused; she was not.

He got to his feet, as well, and captured her face with his palms before she could make her escape. His dancing eyes slowly studied her flushed face.

"Mayhap there is a better way to warm you up," he told her in that throaty voice that made her weak in the knees.

Pasting on a flirtatious smile, she slowly slid her hands up his chest, placing her palms against his rock-hard torso. His eyes widened, his amusement replaced with uncertainty. Taking him unaware, she tucked a leg behind his and shoved against his chest with all her might. She stepped quickly backward as he was caught off balance, flailing the air helplessly before tumbling into the frigid waters of the fjord. The sheer size of him caused the water to surge upward, and Mist had to jump out of the way to avoid being drenched herself. Valdyr came up spluttering and wiping the water from his face. He looked up at her in astonishment, amusement gleaming from his eyes that promised retribution.

Placing her fists against her hips, she shot back, "Mayhap it would be better to cool you off instead."

She hurried back to the safety of the house, his laughter following after.

# *Chapter 12*

$V$aldyr, shivering after his unexpected swim in the fjord, headed straight for the *sowna*. Thankfully, it was bath day, and the small room was already steaming.

His lips twitched as he pictured Mist's amused face. It bothered him more than a little that she had been able to take him unaware, but after kissing her, his mind was foggier than the fjord on a murky day. The stories her father told about her were nothing like the woman he had come to know.

He leaned back against the paneled wall and thought about everything she had said about her God. What could possibly make a powerful Viking warrior who could wield a sword with deadly intent into a sweet, untried maiden? Was it this God of hers? If so, he wasn't willing to follow such a God. He had no desire to be so emasculated.

Mayhap under that quiet exterior she was not quite as

innocent as she seemed. She cared for him; he could see it in her eyes whenever he touched her. But every time he tried to draw her closer, she managed to pull away. He wondered just how much of that had to do with her God.

The men of the farm joined him in the *sowna* inter mittently but, busy with his own thoughts, he didn't join in their conversations. He wondered if he agreed to be baptized, would Mist then act differently toward him?

He could hear the yells of the men who had just left the steam bath as they jumped into the frigid waters of the fjord. Smiling wryly, Valdyr lifted the ladle and poured more water over the hot stones. Hissing steam rose into the air and swirled around his head. Thanks to Mist, the regular order of his bathing ritual—hot first, then cold—had been reversed today.

Bjorn joined him moments later. "I wondered where you had disappeared to."

Valdyr smiled. "I am surprised that you left Astrid's side."

"The women and children are bathing in the house. Egil is inside."

Enough said. Egil might be advanced in years, but even Valdyr would hesitate to challenge the older man in his own home.

Bjorn seated himself next to Valdyr and leaned over the heated rocks to soften his beard. Like many men, Bjorn and Valdyr preferred to keep their beards clipped short around their mouth and chin and shave their cheeks. They did the same with their hair, keeping it close to their neck so that in battle, the hair would not get in their face and blind them.

Wondering if he should warn his brother of Mist's suspicions in regard to Balder's reasons for coming to the farm, he finally decided against it. Having been fore-warned himself, Valdyr would keep a close eye on the two men. He didn't want his brother looking for a reason to start a fight.

Bjorn glanced his way. "Since Egil has given his permission for Astrid and I to marry in the spring, what will that mean for you and Mist?"

Valdyr looked at him. "Nothing has changed, as far as I am concerned. The contract between Egil and I was garnered long ago and would take both of us to change it. Egil has said nothing to me, and I, for my part, see no reason to change it, either."

"And Mist?"

And that was the rub. Would Mist refuse to marry him now?

Valdyr didn't answer his brother, and Bjorn was wise enough to let the matter rest.

Mist found a moment to be alone with Iliana after the woman had taken her bath. She offered to comb her hair while Knut was in the *sowna*. It surprised her that Knut refused to have his wife stay in the barn with him. Mist hadn't believed him capable of such consideration and wondered if she had been wrong about him after all. To travel as far as he had during the cold months of darkness showed at least some concern.

She hadn't missed the fact that Iliana had been subdued ever since her return from walking with Knut.

Remembering her conversation with Valdyr, Mist began to gently untangle Iliana's mass of dark hair. If Knut meant her harm, would he tell Iliana? She asked, "Is everything well with you, Iliana?"

After some moments had passed, she answered on a whisper. "Everything is well."

Mist noticed that she was clutching something in her hand. Separating the dark locks into three pieces, she began a braid. "What have you there?"

"Nothing! It is nothing but a stone!"

Surprise at Iliana's angry reaction rendered Mist speechless. Iliana turned quickly, instantly contrite. "I beg pardon, Mist. I…I am not myself tonight."

That was for certain, and it didn't take a prophet to understand why.

"I didn't mean to pry," Mist soothed.

"I know." She got to her feet after Mist tied the end of the braid. "Thank you for doing my hair."

Mist watched her go to Brita to retrieve her daughter. The two spoke for a moment before Iliana went to feed little Cecilia. What had caused such a violent reaction in the woman? Mist shrugged off her feeling of unease over the matter. If Iliana wanted to share her thoughts, she no doubt would in time.

At the end of the day, after everyone had bathed, Mist asked a couple of the men to empty the tub outside. She would then place it back in its place at the back of the house until next *Lordag*. Tomorrow was *Sondag*, or sun's day. Christians revered it as the Lord's Day. She had spent many such days with Drustan after she had been baptized and recovered from her injuries. The breaking of the bread and sharing of the wine that represented the Lord's body and blood had been a special time for her.

Since her return to the island, she had taken to going to her special place with some bread and wine that she had confiscated from her father's private stock. She longed to hear the words again that Drustan had read to her each Lord's Day from his copy of the Holy Scriptures.

Sighing, she put away the towels and the soap.

Valdyr came into the house and went to his rolled-up sleeping pallet. He picked it up, motioning to two of his men to do the same, and went to retrieve his sword.

Concerned, Mist hurried to his side. "What are you doing?"

"I will be sleeping in the barn tonight," he told her, the inflection in his voice warning her that there would be no gainsaying him. He lifted one of the walrus oil lamps from the table to light his way, careful not to spill the liquid that filled the stone well.

In truth, Mist was relieved. With Valdyr there to watch over Knut and Balder, she would rest easier. And with all of the animals inside, the stable was nearly as warm as the house, so there was no need to be worried about Valdyr freezing.

Valdyr watched as the two men carried the tub the women had bathed in outside to dump its contents. He glanced down at Mist, a sparkle lighting his eyes. "If you have not yet bathed, I know of a convenient location."

Mist pressed her lips tightly together to keep from grinning. She would have moved out of his reach, but she was no coward. Whatever she could dish out to others, she was willing to take on herself.

Valdyr curled his hand behind her neck and lifted her chin with his thumb. The warmth emanating from his eyes once again melted her reticence. Surely if he looked at an iceberg in that manner, it would instantly turn into a puddle of water.

"Do not distress yourself, my sweet," he breathed, and

she felt her face warm at the endearment. "I have something much different planned in retaliation."

He released her and motioned for the two men he had called to follow him. Mist stood there like a frozen ice sculpture for several long moments until Brita called her name.

Valdyr strode to the barn, Amund and Rolf following grudgingly behind him. The landscape was bathed in moonlight from the full moon, making the lamp unnecessary. Their footsteps were muffled by the thin layer of snow that was beginning to settle over the land as a curtain of white flakes fell from the sky.

If he was alone, he would have taken a minute to stop and appreciate the white orb peering through the colorful lights spanning the dark sky. Realizing that his men wouldn't favor standing in the cold while he did so, Valdyr instead made quick work of the distance to the stable.

Reaching the door to the barn, Valdyr jerked it open and quickly ducked inside, his nostrils flaring at the intense smell that assailed him. Grumbling from his men assured him that they were not any more appreciative of the odorous atmosphere than he was.

Whispering from the back of the barn turned to instant silence. The stillness was disturbed only by the cattle shifting uneasily at their intrusion. Moonlight slitting through a crack in the wall showed Knut and Balder as shadows slowly rising to their feet from the straw mound where they had made their bed.

Valdyr lifted the stone lamp, its flickering flame barely penetrating into the darkness beyond. As he moved closer, he could see the surprise on the men's faces. They glanced past his shoulder and saw Amund and Rolf seeking spots to take their rest for the night, their swords glinting from the small flame of the lamp.

Noticing that Valdyr was similarly armed, Knut's expression quickly went from surprise to anger. Valdyr lifted a brow, daring him to say anything.

"Do not let us disturb your rest." Valdyr tossed his blanket on the nearest stack of hay. When he could see that his men were safely ensconced, he blew out the flame of the lamp and settled himself for a long night of surveillance.

He heard Knut and Balder resume their seats, and could feel their tension even from a distance.

His eyes finally adjusting to the darkness, Valdyr stared up at the ceiling. When he heard the snoring of the others, he let his thoughts drift. Inevitably, they turned to Mist.

He grinned to himself as he pictured her stunned expression at his last remark to her. The thought of dunking her in the cold fjord really held no appeal. He turned his attention instead to thinking about the future.

The fact that Bjorn and Astrid were now free to marry changed nothing in his mind. He was determined to make Mist his, and may the heavens help anyone who stood in his way.

That thought brought him up short. Had he just shaken his fist in the face of her God? A coldness that had nothing to do with the outside temperatures shuddered through him. Whether he was willing to worship him or not, he was beginning to respect this God who would give His only Son so that mankind could spend eternity with Him.

"I beg pardon," he whispered into the darkness.

He lay thus, his mind unable to let go of thoughts of Mist and her devotion to her God until light shone beneath the barn door, telling him that the sun had begun its ascent.

He heard Knut and Balder rise and make ready to leave. Allowing them to believe that he still slept, he watched them through slitted eyes as they carefully stepped over him and the others, and made their way outside.

Valdyr quietly opened the door after they had left to see where they went. Not waiting to break the fast, they hurried though the gate of the rock fence that surrounded the farm and disappeared over the hill that led back to Straumfjord.

Valdyr gave a disbelieving snort. So much for Knut being anxious to see his wife and child again.

# Chapter 13

The days began to lengthen, a forewarning that summer would soon be upon them. Each day the sunlight intensified and the grass began to turn green after its winter dormancy.

It would soon be time to shear the sheep and prepare the *vadmal* for trading when the trading ships returned to the island.

Mist, Brita and Edda spent many hours making and packaging extra cheese while the other women carded and spun the remaining wool from last fall's shearing, and then wove it into sheets of material.

Brita was embroidering a new dress for Astrid's upcoming wedding. She and Mist had used the best of the wool to weave the garment and Brita was now adding the finishing touches.

An air of excitement infused the farm. Not only was Astrid's wedding drawing closer, but Finn's family was preparing to head out to the farm Egil had given them, eager to begin their new life. Iliana was shifting supplies in the wagon to make room for the barrel of whale meat that Finn had brought from the storehouse. Mist added a soapstone bowl to the already loaded wagon.

"I wish we had an iron cauldron to spare," she told Iliana regretfully.

Iliana turned to her, a look of surprise on her face. "Do not be foolish! You have given us so much already. We will make do until the traders arrive."

At least they would have something to trade. Finn's family had been responsible for catching and drying nearly as many *skreid* as her own people. And with the cattle that her father had sold Finn, they were able to process at least a few pounds of cheese and butter. Every little bit would help to get them back on their feet.

Astrid came from the house holding little Cecilia. Mist smiled at the picture they made as Astrid tickled the child, and Cecilia's uninhibited laughter filled the air. Astrid reluctantly handed the child to her mother. "I am going to miss you," she told Iliana.

Laughter lit Iliana's eyes. "It is more like you are going to miss my daughter."

Color flowed into Astrid's cheeks. "That is not true. You have become like a sister to us." She turned to Mist. "Hasn't she?"

Mist smiled. "Indeed."

Iliana's face softened. "As have you to me." Iliana then surprised Mist by stepping away from the wagon, her searching gaze swiftly scanning the farm. "Do you know where I may find Valdyr?"

Mist was shocked at the jealousy that swept through

her. What business had Iliana with Valdyr? As far as she knew, they rarely even spoke to each other.

"He and Bjorn went to the boat shed," Astrid told her.

Finn joined them and began tying down the articles in the wagon. "We need to leave soon to make it to the farm before sunset."

Iliana nodded. "I am ready, but I need to do something first."

"Make it quick," Finn told her and went to gather the other members of his clan.

Iliana handed Cecilia back to a surprised Astrid and headed in the direction of the boat shed. Mist watched her go, an unwelcome jealousy coiling through her like a serpent.

Valdyr and Bjorn were investigating their longship in the boatshed for signs of damage. From their inspection, they could see that the ship had weathered the winter remarkably well, and they were both pleased.

Although Valdyr was committed to staying on the island until his wedding in the fall, he yearned to make a short trip out into the ocean once again. Eyes that had forever been looking toward the horizon and had kept him on the move were now turned inward most of the time, keeping him close to a woman whom he was beginning to believe that he loved.

He wasn't certain that he even knew what love was, but he had the feeling that it had crept up on him unexpectedly. If love meant wanting to be with Mist every minute of every day, searching her out whenever he returned from some task, thinking of her first thing when he awoke and last thing before he went to sleep—then he was definitely in love.

"Some of the tar caulking has been lost," Bjorn said, bringing him back to the matter at hand. "We will have to use some *vadmal* and seal oil to replace it."

Valdyr looked up from the boat to see Iliana standing patiently in the open doorway, waiting for them to acknowledge her. Her face reflected her troubled thoughts.

Bjorn rose from his kneeling position and exchanged a quick, surprised look with Valdyr before turning back to Iliana.

"How may we help you, Iliana?"

She looked past Bjorn to Valdyr, and something in her eyes made the hair rise on the back of his neck in forewarning. "I need to speak with Valdyr for a moment before we take our leave."

Valdyr pondered her reason for doing so. He had barely spoken to the woman in the months they had been together. He had the ominous feeling that he wasn't going to like what she had to say.

"Please come in," Valdyr bade her, but she shook her head.

"Alone," she insisted.

Bjorn shared a long look with him. "I will go gather some of the men to work on the ship."

Valdyr nodded his assent, and Iliana waited until Bjorn was gone before turning to Valdyr. She crossed the shed in seeming reluctance, and Valdyr tensed.

She held out a black rock with a carving on it. "A runestone?" he asked in surprise.

Valdyr felt a vague disquiet, wondering why the woman would choose to give him a gift. He knew that many of his people had developed a system of forth telling using carved symbols to guide them in making decisions, but he had never believed in them for himself.

He tried to think of a way, without hurting her feelings, to let her know that he wasn't interested in accepting such a gift.

"It is not a stone for telling the future or guiding decisions," she told him. "Knut gave it to me. It has his name carved on it."

Valdyr reached out to take the stone, even though he was reluctant to touch anything that bore Knut's name. The stone had been warmed by where Iliana had clutched it in her hand. Turning it over, Valdyr found it just as she said.

Lifting an eyebrow, he cocked his head at her. "What has this to do with me?"

"It does not," she answered, wrapping her arms defensively around her waist. "It has to do with Astrid."

A cold chill passed through him, and he frowned. "What about Astrid? And why tell me and not Bjorn?"

She blew out a frustrated breath. "While I do not love my husband, he is Finn and Edda's son and they would be devastated if anything happened to him. If Bjorn thought there was any danger to Astrid, he would seek Knut out and possibly slay him."

"And you think that I will not?" he questioned angrily, already making plans to do just that.

She studied him, as though she could see inside his very soul. "I think that you are more levelheaded," she said quietly.

Her words neutralized his anger and gave him pause. "I would not count too heavily on my forebearance," he warned her.

"Well, I am." She walked to the door, but turned back to face him again. "I do not know what Knut is about. I only know that it cannot be good. He told me to leave this stone at the place where Mist goes to pray if there was news of Astrid's wedding date."

The blood began to heat inside of him at the thought of Knut awaiting Mist at her chosen place of prayer.

"I believe Balder put Knut up to whatever they have planned," Iliana told him. "I could not do as he asked. Mist…" She paused, taking in a quivering breath. "Mist, Astrid and Brita are sisters to me. Maybe not in blood, but in my heart. I would not have anything happen to any of them."

"Nothing will," he promised her. It was a vow he meant to keep.

"You do not know Knut," she cautioned him. "I only wanted to make you aware so that you could keep watch."

As Valdyr watched her leave, he felt a swell of compassion for her, and an equal measure of rage for Knut and Balder. He needed to make Mist aware of the danger, not only to her sister, but to her, as well.

Bjorn joined him moments after Iliana had gone, lifting a brow in question.

"It is nothing," Valdyr told him, and Bjorn allowed the falsehood to pass.

Several of the men joined them, carrying scraps of the *vadmal* and bowls of heated seal oil. Valdyr set Bjorn to the task of overseeing the project while he searched out Mist, his heart pounding with dread when he could not immediately locate her. If the woman had gone to her place of worship, anything might happen to her.

He finally found her at the smithy watching her uncle as he forged a new sword from the iron Valdyr had brought with him. His relief was palpable.

Caught off guard, Mist didn't have time to hide the

emotion that blazed in her eyes at the sight of him before once again pulling on her cool reserve. His heart reacted to the unmasked reaction by tripling its rhythm, but he forced himself to focus on the matter at hand. Her safety came first.

"I need to speak with you," he told her heavily.

## *Chapter 14*

Several days later Astrid told Mist that she wanted to make the trip to Orm the Combmaker's farm. Orm was another of Egil's tenant farmers and was known for his exceptional quality of carved combs.

Mist was busy helping to shear the sheep. Remembering her conversation with Valdyr, she rose to look at her sister, placing one hand at her aching back. "Not alone," she warned. Her sister had a tendency to believe that living on this island so far away from others made it completely safe. Perhaps she should have shared Valdyr's warning with her, but she had been afraid that Astrid would let something slip to Bjorn.

Recognizing Mist's decisive look from many times past, Astrid frowned her irritation. "Will you come with me then?"

Mist blew out a frustrated breath. "Can you not see that we are busy? Why do you want to go?"

"I want to purchase a comb for Bjorn for a wedding gift."

Mist could think of no finer gift but now was not a good time. "Can it not wait?"

A petulant look crossed Astrid's face that Mist also recognized from times past. A battle was about to ensue. To ward it off, Mist suggested, "Take Gudrun with you."

Astrid looked as though she was about to object, but said, "As you wish."

When her sister turned, Mist reminded her, "Do not forget. You have to help with the spinning."

Astrid wrinkled her dainty nose as she walked away. Being the favored daughter, and the youngest, Astrid shirked hard duties whenever possible, but Mist couldn't blame it all on her father. She and Brita had had a hand in it, as well. Shaking her head, Mist turned back to the sheep, picking up her shears.

Hours later, Mist released an exhausted breath and seated herself on the bench beside the barn. Thirty bald sheep now scattered across the *tún*, the dung field that surrounded the farm and was already thick with green verge.

She had a sense of well-being from a job well done. The others who had helped in the shearing waved in farewell as they returned to their other labors. She watched them go, too tired to do more than lift a hand in return.

Her thoughts turned to what was left to be done for Astrid's wedding. Word had been sent out to all the outlying farms. People would come from miles to celebrate not only the wedding, but the spring solstice. The feasting would last for days, and Mist was thankful that they had prepared well in advance, that the winter had been mild and that they were well supplied.

It was why she had instead chosen fall for her own wedding. By then, stocks were always replenished and food was not in short supply.

She pulled herself tiredly to her feet, knowing that there was still much to do before then. The sun was beginning its descent, and darkness would follow quickly.

She entered the house and found Brita busy preparing the evening meal. Glancing around, Mist asked, "Where is Astrid?"

Brita snorted impatiently. "I have not seen her all day. You know if there is work to do she has a tendency to disappear."

Frowning, Mist placed her shears and knife in the wooden storage chest. "She was going to Orm's to purchase a comb early this morning. Has she not returned at all?" Mist noticed that Gudrun was still absent, as well. "Where is Gudrun?"

Brita shook her head, loudly thumping the wooden platters on the table, a clear indication of her irritation at having to do everyone's work.

"She went with Astrid." She glanced at Mist. "Astrid told me that you suggested it."

Mist felt a creeping sense of doom. She should have taken Valdyr's warning more seriously. Truly, she had not believed that Balder would do anything that might cause a blood feud between their families. Her heart picked up pace, and she had to take a deep breath to calm herself so as not to alarm her sister. She was letting her imagination get away with her. But they should have been back long ago.

"I will see if I can find them," she said, and went to

retrieve her sword. First, she would try to locate Valdyr. She had the disturbing feeling that she was going to need his help.

The men found Gudrun unconscious and bound halfway between the farm and Orm's house. When finally freed, she told them that Astrid had been taken by Balder and some of his men. Valdyr saw the set of his brother's face and knew that if they caught up with the others, blood would surely be shed.

Gudrun was in no condition to travel farther, so Mist had to return to the farm with her while Valdyr and Bjorn went on. Only her concern for the other woman had made Mist capitulate. The look of pure rage in her eyes gave even Valdyr pause, but he had his hands full trying to control his brother. Although a fairly large island, it was small enough that a longstanding blood feud would be catastrophic. If there was a way to bring about a peaceful ending to this situation, it would be better for all involved.

Valdyr was reluctant to leave Mist on her own, but he could see no way around it. He picked Gudrun up and placed her on Mist's horse, thankful they had chosen to use the animals as time was of the essence. Since the others were on foot, they had a better chance of catching them.

He caught Mist by the arm as she turned away. "Be careful!"

Her face softened at his concern, her beautiful green eyes reflecting his own anxiety. Nodding, she took the reins and waited for him to leave.

Valdyr could feel her eyes boring into his back as he and Bjorn kicked their horses into a gallop.

When they reached Balder's farm, the light was already beginning to dim from the retreating sun. They slowly dismounted as a man he assumed to be Balder's father came out of his house to greet them. He studied them, his glance resting briefly on their swords before landing on their faces.

"Greetings," he called, a question in the tone of his voice.

"Where is she?" Bjorn demanded, and Valdyr put out a hand to hold him back.

Folding his massive arms across his chest, the man inquired in a deceptively mild voice, "Who are you?"

It was easy to see where Balder got his great height. Like Finn, this man, though past his prime, was not one to be trifled with.

"I am Valdyr, and this is my brother, Bjorn. We have come from Egilsfjord."

"I am Ragnar. What is it you wish of me?"

"Your son Balder has taken the daughter of Egil Half-stanson. We have come to get her back."

A look of distress crossed Ragnar's face. "I did not know." He motioned for them to come into his house, but Valdyr shook his head. He was taking no chance that they were walking into an ambush.

"My son is not here," Ragnar told them, recognizing Valdyr's reluctance.

"You lie!" Bjorn growled, stepping forward and pulling his sword from its scabbard.

Fire lit the old man's brown eyes. Although unarmed, he was unfazed by Bjorn's threatening posture.

"I do not lie," Ragnar returned, his voice holding a warning of its own. "Balder has left the island to return to Norway. He and Knut both." The look he gave

Valdyr was apologetic. "I truly did not know. I saw no woman with them."

Valdyr believed him, but he wasn't certain that Egil would be so understanding.

"How long ago did they leave?" he asked.

Ragnar sighed, looking even more apologetic. "Several hours I am afraid."

Bjorn was on the verge of violence, and Valdyr couldn't blame him. Had they taken Mist, there was no telling what he might have done himself.

"Bjorn, put away your sword," Valdyr commanded, and his brother reluctantly complied. Valdyr turned his attention back to Ragnar. "I need to know where they will go."

Ragnar nodded. The man fully grasped the repercussions of such an act. Major conflicts had been started over less, leaving behind a bloody aftermath.

"Come inside and I will show you a map to our home in Norway."

Valdyr gave the man the benefit of the doubt and followed him inside. Bjorn was close behind him, his hand resting on his sword. They paused just inside the doorway to allow their eyes to adjust to the dim light.

Ragnar went to a chest in the corner and pulled out a sheet of vellum and spread it across the table. Valdyr studied it, noting that it was well drawn up, probably by a scribe. He recognized many of the farms listed, including his father's.

Ragnar pointed to a place on the map that was very close to his father's. "Here. This is our home." He saw the recognition on Valdyr's face. "You know it?"

Valdyr nodded, but refrained from mentioning that Ragnar's family and his own were embroiled in a land dispute of their own. No doubt the other man would not take kindly to the information.

"I am familiar with that part of Norway."

He and Bjorn shared a look over Ragnar's head, and Valdyr imperceptibly shook his head in warning.

Valdyr straightened. "We appreciate your help," he told Ragnar.

"Were it my daughter, I would feel the same." Sadness crossed Ragnar's face. "Please assure Egil that I had no knowledge of my son's actions. Whatever *wergild* he decides on, I will gladly pay."

"If any harm comes to Astrid," Valdyr warned, "I do not think you will like hearing the judgment."

Ragnar met his look, his nostrils flaring as he sucked in a sharp breath. He nodded. "Do what you must."

## Chapter 15

Valdyr blew out a frustrated breath. He had searched everywhere for Mist but could not locate her anywhere around the farm. Her sword was gone, as well, so he reasoned that she must have gone inland to pray for her sister.

Maddening woman! He had hoped to speak with her before they left, assure her that they would return. Now, he could wait no longer. Time was against them. They needed to put to sail before Balder got too much of a head start. As it was, Bjorn was on the verge of leaving him behind.

They made their way to where the men had put the ship in the water. Valdyr kept searching as they walked along, but he still saw no sign of Mist. Not paying attention to where he was going, he slammed into his brother's back.

"What are you about?" Valdyr growled, stepping

around his brother's still figure. Seeing the look of astonishment on Bjorn's face, Valdyr followed the direction of his gaze.

Mist stood in the prow of his ship, but a Mist almost unrecognizable. She was dressed in men's leggings and a short tunic, her long red hair hanging over one shoulder in a braid that reached to her waist. Her sword hung in its baldric crosswise over her chest, the exposed metal glinting in the early morning light.

Valdyr stared at her in amazement. He had tried to imagine her thus, but his mental image had failed utterly compared to the figure he was seeing before him now. She fairly took his breath away.

His astonishment lasted but a moment, quickly replaced by fury as he realized what her presence here, dressed thus, meant. He closed the space between them in a few rapid strides.

"No! You are not going with us."

He soon realized that his anger was nothing in comparison to hers. Her eyes glimmered with a rage that told him he had a battle on his hands if he hoped to make her see reason.

She slowly drew her sword from its sheath, the metal gliding against the baldric with an ominous hissing sound. "Then you will have to remove me from this ship," she told him, her voice threateningly low. "If you can."

His men slowly began to move to positions where they would be able to overtake her, but he motioned them to stillness. This was between the two of them.

"Your father needs you here," he reasoned, slowly moving closer.

"My sister needs me more," she rebutted, arcing her sword until it whistled through the air.

There was a part of him that wanted to take on her challenge, that part of him that felt the need to bring his enemies into subjection. The other part of him, the more sane part, knew that although he could disarm her, it would not be without injury, and he had no desire to see her hurt.

Egil's voice coming from behind him settled the matter.

"She is going."

The finality of his voice left no room for argument. Valdyr wanted to object, but he could see purpose behind the decision. When they found Astrid, *if* they found Astrid, she would need a woman's comforting arms. Even Bjorn, as much as he loved Astrid, would not be able to understand as a woman would.

Valdyr saw the look that passed between father and daughter. "As you wish," he told them, not feeling the same confidence he saw in them.

For a moment, no one moved, then Bjorn stepped forward and began barking out orders. The men warily eyed Mist as they jumped into the ship to prepare to set sail.

Mist gave an inward sigh of relief, thankful that her father had spoken up. In reality, she had no desire to go against Valdyr in a sword fight. She had watched him sparring with his men and knew that he had an instinctive skill that would make him a deadly foe. Her own skill was no match for his.

She seated herself in the middle of the ship. Valdyr ignored her, moving among the men and giving commands as they maneuvered out of the fjord and into the open sea.

Mist settled herself in for a long voyage. There would be no stopping this time, and there would be no privacy except what the men afforded her. If not for Valdyr, she might have been a little concerned knowing from past experience that such close confines could make for embarrassing moments.

Valdyr stood with Bjorn in the fore of the ship. They were in deep discussion, searching the horizon for any signs of a ship although they knew that it was doubtful they would spot one. Balder had more than half a day's start on them.

Leaving Bjorn to watch the ocean, Valdyr came and seated himself beside Mist. She shifted uncomfortably under his intense look.

"What do you plan to do if we catch up with them?" he asked. "I thought slaying was against this faith of yours."

She didn't pretend to misunderstand him. "I am not here to slay anyone. I am here for my sister."

He glanced askance at her sword and lifted a brow in question. It was clear that he doubted her word. Frankly, she doubted herself. Trepidation made her stomach suddenly queasy.

"I will do what is necessary," she told him firmly. "Although I am praying to God that I will not be called upon to slay anyone."

She hoped that she was telling the truth, because that old nature that the apostle Paul spoke about was struggling for supremacy, and it wanted vengeance.

He studied her a moment with his head cocked to

the side. Surprisingly, she saw amusement twitching at his lips.

"Perhaps you should add to your prayers that the winds be with us instead of against us."

She looked up in surprise and saw that the men had lowered the sail and were rowing hard against the prevailing winds. Their muscles that had softened over the winter were straining against the oars.

Was that a challenge she saw in his blue eyes? "I will do so," Mist told him and bowed her head to do just that. When she opened her eyes again, Valdyr had moved back to Bjorn's side.

A short time later, the wind shifted directions and a cool sea breeze suddenly sprang up from behind them. Valdyr threw Mist a look that was hard to interpret, barking a quick command for the sail to be lifted, and the men hurried to hoist it up. Those men seated near Mist stared at her in uneasy amazement. They had to have heard the conversation between her and Valdyr and knew that she had prayed to God, but even Mist was amazed at the rapid response to her prayer. The hope that God was on their side grew, dimming the rage running through her.

Time seemed to pass slowly even though they were making quick progress, but the monotonous hours on the sea were wearing on Mist's already raw nerves. The thought of what could be happening to her sister made her antsy, frustrated that Astrid's fate was beyond her control.

Their second day out, Mist saw Valdyr pointing off to the northeast. She saw a low cloud bank on the distant horizon and a cold shudder racked through her that had nothing to do with the chill of the air. Well she knew the danger of a storm at sea. It wouldn't be her first, but she was certain it would be no less frightening. A man with a sword you could predict and possibly overcome; not so the sea.

She threw up a prayer that the storm system was moving away from them, but that prayer was not answered in the way she had hoped. It was a fast-moving storm, the swelling and surging of the sea their first indication of its rapid approach.

Valdyr called for the sail to be dropped and the oars to be pulled in, and everyone prepared to ride out what was going to be a ferocious storm. Mist was thankful that Valdyr's ship had higher sides, a second deck and extra trusses, which would make it better able to handle the rough seas, but she knew if the waves were too high, they might possibly all lose their lives. She began a prayer that would not end until they were out of danger...or she went to meet her Lord.

Valdyr took some rope and wound it around his waist, then wrapped it around hers, as well. She tried to meet his worried look with one of complete confidence, but too well she knew the horrors of being in such weather on the open sea. He pulled her close with one arm, and she allowed herself to lean against him, placing one hand against his chest where she could feel the comforting rhythm of his beating heart.

The storm came with fiercely crashing waves, drenching everyone in the ship. Darkness surrounded them, shutting out the normal light of day and the stars that would guide them by night. Hour upon hour they tossed on the relentless sea.

Mist huddled in Valdyr's arms as he tried to protect her from the worst of the rain and wind. He whispered something into her ear, but the howling gale tore the words away. She leaned her head back against his arm and met his eyes, those vivid blue eyes that invaded her dreams, and even her waking thoughts. He lifted a hand to her face, trailing his fingers softly against her wet cheek. Her look invited him to kiss her, and he readily complied. After that, the cold ocean water stood no chance against the warmth that flooded through her.

For two days they weathered the storm before it finally passed and daylight once again returned. By that time, they had been blown off course and were seemingly lost at sea.

Valdyr loosened the rope from around them. He made his way to the front of the ship and studied the sun at its horizon line. He gave a sharp command to put up the sail with the wind to their back.

Mist joined him at the prow of the ship, shivering in her wet garments. The others seemed impervious to the cold wind blowing against their wet clothing.

"Do you know where we are?" she asked, searching for a landmark, but all that met her eyes wherever she turned was the sea.

"Not for certain, but I have an idea."

Mist didn't see how he could possibly know where they were when they were surrounded by nothing but water.

"Where do you think we are?"

He cast an eye over the sky and the water around them. "I believe we are close to Hedeby."

"Hedeby!" she said, appalled. "Then we are too far south!"

He nodded agreement, but continued to search for some sign of land. Mist blew breath through her pinched lips. There was really nothing she could do but trust that her God had everything under control.

It was hard to describe to someone unused to the sea, but the water had a different feel in different locations. Valdyr sensed that they were close to the waters around Hedeby.

The men let out a cheer when they spotted white clouds in the distance, because clouds formed over land and that meant that they were close to shore. The question was, was it indeed Hedeby, or were they even farther south into more hostile territory?

Bjorn joined him and Mist. They watched tensely as the ship drew closer to the land. Suddenly Bjorn's shoulders relaxed. "It is the inlet to Hedeby."

Valdyr nodded and decided to land there and replenish his supplies before heading for Norway. It was possible that Balder's ship was blown off course, as well. It could very well be that they were even here at Hedeby.

Several men were left to guard the ship while the others, along with Bjorn, made their way through the town to find out if Balder was in the vicinity.

Valdyr and Mist went in the opposite direction. The stench of rotting meat filled the air where the people had offered sacrifices to the gods and had hung them outside their houses and places of business. Hawkers bid them to come investigate their wares. Children ran up and down the streets chasing dogs, pigs and chickens. The sights and sounds of the town would have been intriguing at any other time, but Mist was obviously focused on more important things.

When she saw a figure in monk's clothing hurrying

down the street, she stopped midstride, her eyes going wide with recognition.

"Drustan!"

Valdyr had but a second to grasp her arm before she could take off after the fast-disappearing man. "Wait!" he commanded.

"Let go!" she growled, and jerking free from his grasp, she ran after the quickly vanishing figure, yelling his name as she tried to overtake him.

The monk stopped, looking around in puzzlement. He spotted Mist running toward him and his surprised face creased into a welcoming smile.

Valdyr took in the man even before he reached him. He was small but robust for his apparent age. Wrinkles covered every inch of his face and even part of his bald pate. There was kindness in the faded eyes that finally made Valdyr pause.

Mist threw herself into the old man's arms and burst into tears. He patted her uncertainly on the back, his face a picture of confusion.

When Valdyr joined them, Drustan tensed and tugged Mist closer, his fist tightening around the staff that he carried. Despite the fact that the old man was clenching the stick, Valdyr gave a snort at the thought of being injured by the puny thing. His glare warned the monk not to even try.

Still sniffling, Mist pulled back from the monk's arms and turned to Valdyr to introduce them. When Drustan realized that Valdyr was a friend and not a foe, he relaxed, a friendly twinkle once again warming his eyes.

"What are you doing here, Mist? I thought you had returned to Iceland."

Mist brushed the tears from her cheeks. "I did. I

haven't time to explain everything, but I am seeking information."

She explained about Astrid, describing her in detail, and asked if he might have seen her. "She would be hard to miss. She is very beautiful."

A peculiar look crossed the monk's face. "Come with me. I have something to show you."

They clove their way through the busy market streets until they came to the church that had been built some years before. Valdyr stared at the impressive building curiously. He had heard that since Hedeby was a trading center people from all over the world had settled here. Christians had been allowed, for the most part, to live in peace.

Drustan led them inside. Dozens of candles lit even the darkest corner of the interior. The place was eerily quiet, their footsteps sounding loud against the rushes on the floor as they passed by the empty benches where the worshippers usually sat.

They followed him to a back room shrouded in darkness except for a lone candle next to a wooden bed. There was a figure lying on the bed, a wolfskin pelt covering the small, shivering form.

Mist rushed to the bed, dropping to her knees beside it.

"Astrid!"

Her hands fluttered helplessly over the girl like a butterfly afraid to light. She turned to the monk, her brows drawn down in puzzlement. "How...I don't understand. What's wrong with her? How is she here?"

Drustan folded his arms inside the sleeves of his robe and came to stand beside her. "Slavers from Byzantium were selling her in the marketplace. I purchased her from them."

Confused by the sudden turn of events, it took Vladyr a moment to fully grasp what the man had just said. How had Astrid wound up in the hands of slavers from Byzantium? Quick anger surged through him. He stepped forward and grasped the monk by the front of his tunic. "She is no man's thrall," he growled.

Drustan looked upward in astonishment, his arms hanging limply at his sides. "What? No, No!"

Mist rose quickly to her feet and placed a restraining hand on Valdyr's arm. "Hold, Valdyr. Release him." Her voice held a distinct warning. "Drustan purchases slaves when he can and then gives them their freedom."

Valdyr glanced from one to the other in amazement. The price of slaves was not cheap, especially with raiders from Byzantium. "Why would he do such a thing?" he asked skeptically.

The old man gave him an understanding smile. "It was no less than what my Lord has done for me," Drustan replied softly, and Valdyr stood frozen in indecision, his mind unable to understand such sacrifice. He finally released the man's cloak. Drustan shook out the wrinkles, giving him a cautious glance.

"Were there others with her?" Mist asked anxiously.

Valdyr had almost forgotten about Knut and Balder.

"No," Drustan told her, "there were no others."

Mist didn't know what to think. Had Balder changed his mind and sold Astrid to the Arabic traders? She found that hard to believe. Had their ship then been attacked, and, if so, what had happened to the others? Right now only her sister could answer those questions.

She turned back to the bed. Settling herself on the side of the wooden frame, she pushed the lank blond hair back from her sister's face, which was hot with fever.

"She is ill," Mist stated.

"Which is why the raiders were willing to sell her to me. They were afraid she would die otherwise."

Drustan came and stood beside her, handing her the bowl of water and linen cloth that was sitting on the table. Mist began to gently wipe her sister's face.

"Did she say what happened to the others she was with?"

Drustan shook his head. "I gather from the raiders that they found her floating in the sea on a piece of flotsam."

Valdyr and Mist exchanged an understanding look. The storm must have wrecked Balder's ship. Mist wondered if anyone else had survived, and how long her sister had been in the cold sea.

"Her story is an amazing one," Drustan said, "but understandable now that I know she is your sister."

Mist looked up in surprise. "How so?"

Drustan placed a hand on Mist's shoulder, and she felt the comfort of his touch. "You are God's child, Mist. Surely you prayed for your sister?"

Mist couldn't begin to sort out the feelings that his words brought to mind. Even in her doubts, God was watching out for her, listening to her. She remembered a scripture that Drustan had read to her long ago.

*We also glory in our sufferings, because we know that suffering produces perseverance; perseverance, character; and character, hope.*

That scripture had so much more meaning for her now.

Valdyr interrupted her thoughts. "I need to find Bjorn and the others."

Nodding, Mist barely registered when he left the room. She continued to cool her sister's fevered brow with water and began to pray.

Drustan stood quietly behind her, sensing her need to petition God and adding his own prayers in a soft whisper.

Astrid's eyes fluttered open, then widened in surprise. "Mist?" she croaked.

"I am here, Astrid," she comforted, and took her sister's hand.

"I knew you would come," she whispered hoarsely. "I prayed to your God, Mist. I asked Him to save me."

A tidal wave of joy rushed through Mist at her sister's confession. Were the seeds she had planted at last bearing fruit? "And He did, *elskling*," she returned softly, forcing the words past the lump in her throat.

Bjorn rushed into the room, pausing just inside the doorway. Seeing Astrid, he ran to her side, sliding to his knees beside her.

"Astrid!" he whispered. She reached for him, and he cautiously took her hand as though afraid she might break. He looked to Mist for permission, and she nodded her head, rising from her seat to give them some privacy. Bjorn took her place on the side of the bed and carefully folded Astrid into his arms.

Valdyr stood in the doorway, and Mist joined him. They both glanced at the couple, but quickly looked away, their eyes connecting in a look of complete understanding.

"How is she?" he asked.

Still overcome with emotion, she smiled widely. "I think she will be fine."

Drustan motioned them out of the room. They followed him to another room that contained a table and four chairs and seated themselves while Drustan collected a platter of bread and cheese and set it before them.

"You must be hungry. Eat," he admonished, seating himself across from her. "It has been a long time, Mist."

Indeed, it had. Too long. "I have missed you, Drustan."

"And I, you."

He glanced at Valdyr and waited for the explanation she had been reluctant to give earlier.

"Valdyr is my betrothed," she told him, and found that the words did not choke her as they once had. The thought of belonging to him no longer held the terror that had filled her earlier in their relationship.

The two men took each other's measure and seemed to approve, though with reservations.

"And is Valdyr a Christian?"

She had known that he was going to ask that. Embarrassed, Mist reached for a piece of cheese to keep from meeting the old man's eyes.

"I would like to be," Valdyr stated quietly, and Mist choked on the bite of bread she had just taken. Valdyr reached across and thumped her on the back, making her eyes water even more.

Drustan was looking at Valdyr in an odd way. "For Mist?" he asked warily, and Mist held her breath, awaiting his answer.

Valdyr looked into her eyes, and she saw a softness there that she had never seen before. "At one time I would have said yes."

"But now?" Drustan inquired.

"Now," he said, still staring intently into her eyes.

"Now I have seen for myself the great power and love that this God has for His people. There is still much I do not understand, but I am willing to learn."

Looking relieved, Drustan sat back in his seat. "You will need to be baptized," he told Valdyr, and Valdyr nodded.

Mist didn't think her body could contain such joy. It felt as though her heart was going to burst from happiness. She felt like lifting her voice and shouting to the skies.

"All things work together for the good of those who are in Christ Jesus," Drustan reminded her, seeing the elation on her face. Her lips quivered with emotion when he met her look in complete understanding. This must be what it was like for Drustan when someone he had been teaching came to understand the love of God.

Valdyr took her hand and raised it to his lips to press a kiss upon it. "I love you," he said in that throaty voice of his, and Mist felt hot color heat her cheeks at the flame that ignited in his eyes. She glanced at Drustan, who was leaning back in his chair, smiling serenely.

She met Valdyr's eyes again, and her heart began to race. "I love you, as well," she answered quietly, finally free to tell him so.

If not for Drustan sitting nearby, she had no doubt from the look in Valdyr's eyes he would have taken her in his arms. Her heart began beating like a wild thing in response.

"When we get back to Iceland, we will be married in the spring instead of waiting for the fall," he directed, but then quickly tacked on, "if that is all right with you."

Mist hid a grin. She knew it would always be thus with a man like Valdyr. He was a man who was meant to command. Before, she would have bristled at such action; now, she felt only cherished and protected.

"If you would allow, my lord," she answered. "I would prefer to be married here by Drustan."

Drustan glanced at her in surprise, his face creasing into a wide smile. "I would be honored," he told her softly.

She saw Valdyr's frown and felt suddenly uncertain.

"You are certain?" he asked. "I thought with your father being *godar*…"

He left the thought unfinished, and Mist shook her head. As main chieftain of their family, her father acted as *godar*, or priest, and he still clung tenaciously to the old ways. Ever since her father had informed her of her forthcoming nuptials, she had tried to think of some way of obeying without participating in a pagan rite. Her God had taken care of even that.

"No. My father would wish to have a pagan ceremony with sacrifices."

A look of understanding crossed Valdyr's face. "So be it. Drustan it is."

Drustan got to his feet, rubbing his palms together. "Let us then see to the matter of your baptism."

When he left the room to make arrangements, Valdyr stood and pulled Mist into his arms. Palms against his chest, she could feel his heart matching hers in a furious rhythm. They searched each other's eyes for a long moment before Valdyr's gaze settled on her lips.

"I think I loved you the moment I laid eyes on you standing on that hill," he told her, his voice husky with emotion.

Mist thought back to that moment and realized that the statement applied to her, as well. There had been some strange kind of bond from the moment their eyes had connected, though in the following months she had fought fiercely with herself to deny it.

He kissed her then, a kiss, but more than a kiss, a seal of possession that she no longer dreaded but actually reveled in. She belonged to him, and he to her.

# *Epilogue*

Mist's wedding was unlike anything she had been expecting. There was no crowd of celebrants, no performing of a sacrifice and no elaborate rites. The only witnesses were her sister, Bjorn and Valdyr's men, who had actually bathed for the occasion even though it was not bath day.

Mist had waited until the fever left her sister and Astrid was on the mend. Astrid stood beside Bjorn now, pale but as beautiful as ever. Bjorn's arm was wrapped possessively around her waist as though he would never let her out of his sight again.

Mist and Valdyr stood before Drustan while he read to them words of scripture in their own language from the scrolls he had been translating. It amazed Mist that the scriptures contained words about husbands and wives, and she wondered what other pearls of wisdom the book contained. She longed to search them for herself.

"'Wives, submit yourselves to your own husbands, as you do to the Lord. For the husband is the head of the wife as Christ is the head of the church, his body, of which he is the Savior. Now as the church submits to Christ, so also wives should submit to their husbands in everything.'"

Mist felt a moment's disquiet. It was not in her nature to be submissive, yet the words spoken so quietly and reverently reached deep into her soul and brought her a peace that let her know that this was where God had intended her to be all along. She and Valdyr would be one flesh, and he would be the head. The thought no longer alarmed her.

Drustan turned his look on Valdyr. "'Husbands, love your wives, just as Christ loved the church and gave himself up for her to make her holy, cleansing her by the washing with water through the word, and to present her to himself as a radiant church, without stain or wrinkle or any other blemish, but holy and blameless.'"

Valdyr reached out and took her hand, clinging to it as Drustan continued.

"'In this same way, husbands ought to love their wives as their own bodies. He who loves his wife loves himself.'"

When Mist met Valdyr's eyes, she knew that he would have an easier time with the command spoken to him, than she with hers. The love shining from his eyes made her feel cherished beyond measure.

"Do you have a ring?" Drustan asked.

Valdyr snapped the silver Thor's hammer necklace hanging from his neck and handed it to Drustan. "Will this do?"

Drustan took the talisman gingerly in his fingers and set it aside. Reaching inside his robe, he pulled out the gold cross that hung around his neck and, lifting it over his head, handed it to Valdyr in its stead.

Valdyr's mouth hung open in astonishment. The look on his face told Mist that he was about to refuse, but Drustan folded Valdyr's large hand around the necklace. They saw in his face that Drustan would never allow Mist to be encumbered with such a pagan talisman and was willing to once again sacrifice something of great worth for someone he loved.

Humbly accepting the sacrifice in the manner it was given, Valdyr then placed the cross around Mist's neck.

Honored by such a gesture, Mist wanted to give Valdyr something of equal worth. She pulled her sword from its sheath and, turning it up in her palms, handed it to him in return.

The expression in his eyes let her know that he understood the meaning behind the gift. She was giving him her most prized possession and turning over her very life to him.

"As you have exchanged these tokens pledging your troth, so now I pronounce you husband and wife. What God has joined together, let no man separate." Drustan smiled at their hesitation as they wondered what came next. There would be no *brudhlap*, nor jumping a broom.

"As a final seal to your vows, you may kiss your bride."

Valdyr willingly complied with a fervor that brought a choking cough from Drustan, and a loud cheer from the men. The thrill that rushed through her as his lips met hers told Mist that she would never get enough of his kisses if she lived to be a hundred years old.

When Valdyr finally pulled back, Drustan continued reading from his scroll. "'Be very careful, then, how you live—not as unwise but as wise, making the most of every opportunity, because the days are evil. Therefore do not be foolish, but understand what the Lord's will is.'"

Drustan placed a hand on each of their shoulders. "May God be with you always, my children."

Mist realized that the time of their parting had come again, and she didn't want to leave. As much as she loved her family, Drustan held the words of life, and there was no one in Iceland who could teach them to her.

"Come with us," she begged the old man, clutching his arm. "Come with us to Iceland."

He pulled back in surprise. "I...I couldn't. I have work to do here." She saw a moment's hesitation in his eyes and pressed her advantage.

"But you are needed there," she pleaded. "Drustan, we have no one."

He cupped her cheek gently with his wrinkled hand, and stared a long moment into her pleading eyes. As though coming to a decision, he sighed regretfully.

"I cannot come with you now, but I will come after I have made arrangements for someone to take my place here."

He reached inside his robe and pulled out a roll of manuscripts and handed them to her. "In the meantime, you can share these with your people."

Mist took the manuscripts, handling them as though they were gold. She wanted to force the issue. She knew that she could by using Drustan's feelings for her, but she could not do that to him. He had made his decision, and it would have to do.

Valdyr took her by the arm. "We must leave now. The tide is about to recede."

Mist reluctantly turned to go. Drustan went with them

to where the ship waited. He stood on the shore as they cast off, and Mist stood in the back of the boat with Valdyr by her side, watching until she could no longer see Drustan, and Hedeby disappeared from their sight.

Sucking in a deep breath to hold back the tears, she didn't resist when Valdyr took her in his arms and held her close.

"I love you," he whispered, and suddenly, that was all that mattered. They were no longer two, but one, and they would raise their children to know the one true God. And maybe, someday, the seeds that they sowed would bear fruit and Iceland would become a Christian nation.

\* \* \* \* \*

# REQUEST YOUR FREE BOOKS!

## 2 FREE INSPIRATIONAL NOVELS
## PLUS 2
# FREE
## MYSTERY GIFTS

*Love Inspired*

# HISTORICAL
INSPIRATIONAL HISTORICAL ROMANCE

# REQUEST YOUR FREE BOOKS!

## 2 FREE RIVETING INSPIRATIONAL NOVELS
## PLUS 2 FREE MYSTERY GIFTS

*Love Inspired*®
# SUSPENSE

---

**YES!** Please send me 2 FREE Love Inspired® Suspense novels and my 2 FREE mystery gifts (gifts are worth about $10). After receiving them, if I don't wish to receive any more books, I can return the shipping statement marked "cancel." If I don't cancel, I will receive 4 brand-new novels every month and be billed just $4.74 per book in the U.S. or $5.24 per book in Canada. That's a savings of at least 21% off the cover price. It's quite a bargain! Shipping and handling is just 50¢ per book in the U.S. and 75¢ per book in Canada.* I understand that accepting the 2 free books and gifts places me under no obligation to buy anything. I can always return a shipment and cancel at any time. Even if I never buy another book, the two free books and gifts are mine to keep forever.

123/323 IDN F5AN

Name _____ (PLEASE PRINT) _____

Address _____ Apt. # _____

City _____ State/Prov. _____ Zip/Postal Code _____

Signature (if under 18, a parent or guardian must sign)

**Mail to the Harlequin® Reader Service:**
**IN U.S.A.:** P.O. Box 1867, Buffalo, NY 14240-1867
**IN CANADA:** P.O. Box 609, Fort Erie, Ontario L2A 5X3

**Are you a current subscriber to Love Inspired Suspense books**
**and want to receive the larger-print edition?**
**Call 1-800-873-8635 or visit www.ReaderService.com.**

\* Terms and prices subject to change without notice. Prices do not include applicable taxes. Sales tax applicable in N.Y. Canadian residents will be charged applicable taxes. Offer not valid in Quebec. This offer is limited to one order per household. Not valid for current subscribers to Love Inspired Suspense books. All orders subject to credit approval. Credit or debit balances in a customer's account(s) may be offset by any other outstanding balance owed by or to the customer. Please allow 4 to 6 weeks for delivery. Offer available while quantities last.

**Your Privacy**—The Harlequin® Reader Service is committed to protecting your privacy. Our Privacy Policy is available online at www.ReaderService.com or upon request from the Harlequin Reader Service.
We make a portion of our mailing list available to reputable third parties that offer products we believe may interest you. If you prefer that we not exchange your name with third parties, or if you wish to clarify or modify your communication preferences, please visit us at www.ReaderService.com/consumerchoice or write to us at Harlequin Reader Service Preference Service, P.O. Box 9062, Buffalo, NY 14269. Include your complete name and address.

# *ReaderService*.com

## Manage your account online!

- Review your order history
- Manage your payments
- Update your address

---

*We've designed
the Harlequin® Reader Service
website just for you.*

---

## Enjoy all the features!

- Reader excerpts from any series
- Respond to mailings and
  special monthly offers
- Discover new series available to you
- Browse the Bonus Bucks catalog
- Share your feedback

*Visit us at:*
# ReaderService.com